Table of Contents

To Mom, who taught me the magic of Christmas.

Chapter One

December 23

S ome may have called Kate Buckner biased, but she believed no one on planet Earth did Christmas better than the small town of Miller's Point, Texas. Okay, she was *totally* biased. After living there her whole life—almost twenty-seven years—she was allowed to love it, especially at this time of year. Miller's Point was a special place all year round, but it had a glow of its own once the weather turned chilly. Yes, even Texas got chilly, though Miller's Point accentuated the natural winter wind with more fake snow and crystal icicles than anywhere else in the world.

The town's glow was only *partly* due to the lights strung around the town square's famous Christmas tree. The rest came from the twinkling of thousands of others decorating every building in town.

Kate crouched precariously atop an eleven-foot ladder, her boots covering the "DANGER—DO NOT STAND ON TOP LEVEL" sticker. Her thighs burned as she reached out for her target… *Just a little further… A little more…*

"Hey!"

Kate froze atop the ladder. Even the subtlest of starts would send the ladder tipping, and she did *not* want to explain to Doctor Bennett how she cracked her skull open. Without moving anything but her eyes, she braved a glance down towards the cobblestones making up Main Street. In just a few hours, they would be covered in fake snow, but for now, they cleaned up nice, sparkling from last night's rainfall. The familiarly muddy boots of Carolyn Bishop, however, ruined the perfect cleanliness—and Kate's view. Kate would've smiled if she hadn't been deathly afraid the slight movement of muscles would send her toppling down to the cold, hard ground.

Her official job title was "Director of Festival Operations," but everyone called her Miss Carolyn, and for good reason. With her eternally good-natured smile and cracked skin testifying to how long she'd been living here, everyone generally considered her the town matriarch. The silver-haired woman with narrowed brown eyes stood lower than five-foot-nothing, but her presence towered over Miller's Point. Kate loved her almost as much as she feared her, which explained the slamming of her heart when she heard the worried accusation in Miss Carolyn's voice.

"What are you doing up there?"

"This light is out!"

Kate stretched her fingers. She was so close, and

if she could only just reach... She grabbed hold of a tiny bulb and twisted it. Once, twice, three times. *There.* The light flickered on, joining the rest of its illuminated brethren on the thick green cord. It was only one piece of a very, very large puzzle, but Kate felt that the little details made all the difference. Miss Carolyn, for her part, didn't share Kate's enthusiasm for tiny lightbulbs or women who put themselves in dangerous situations to fix them.

"You've got to be the most hardheaded girl in town! Get down here before you fall and break your neck! No, you know what? A fall might actually do you some good. Maybe it'd knock some sense into you!"

As she made her way down the ladder, Kate couldn't help but survey the square surrounding her. She would never joke about something as important as Christmas, but she definitely wasn't kidding about the grandeur of Miller's Point. Every year, The Christmas Company—an event planning firm that was a subsidiary of Woodward Enterprises, the corporation that owned most of the ranching operations out here—transformed Miller's Point from one of the countless flyover Texas towns into a Dickensian Christmas wonderland. The square received a makeover, with Hollywood-style facades and enough fake snow to make their humble streets look so much like Victorian London that even a time traveler couldn't have told the difference.

From the day after Thanksgiving until New Year's Eve, the town banded together to host the Miller's

Point Christmas Festival, where guests from all over the country flocked to join in the celebration. Everyone enjoyed the caroling and costumes, but the highlight of the festival—the real reason everyone went—was the immersive reenactment of *A Christmas Carol*. Every night, guests could follow Scrooge on his journey and watch him change from a bitter, hateful miser into a man with the spirit of the season coursing through his veins like an injection of sugarplum juice.

Their town square hosted such scenes as the Ghost of Christmas Present's journey through London and the final celebration after Scrooge's transformation. The Christmas Company spared no expense or labor in making it a dreamscape of holiday fantasy. Paintings on Christmas cards and backdrops in Bing Crosby movies couldn't compare. Lush green garlands wrapped in red ribbons adorned the storefronts covered in fake snow and frost. Countless fairy lights illuminated wreaths and holly, ornaments and decorations of every size and description. Outdoor lanterns and lampposts blazed. No matter where a visitor turned to look, the town simply glowed. It was the perfect backdrop for Tiny Tim to sit on Scrooge's shoulder and shout, "God bless us, everyone," and no matter how hard she tried to remain professional, Kate always cried when they got to that part.

When she finally set her feet on solid ground, Kate braced herself for an earful from Miss Carolyn. After volunteering with the festival since she was seven years old, Kate graduated to full-time employee status at nineteen, the youngest person ever hired by The Christmas Company, and as Assistant of Festival Operations, her list of duties was as extensive as it was satisfying. She ran into trouble, though, with her enthusiasm. As a volunteer, she scrambled to make herself useful, invaluable. Now, as an employee, she always found herself trying to do everything, a habit her boss hated. Miss Carolyn wanted her at her side, not off fixing the hem of Mrs. Cratchit's costume or refilling the mulled wine in Fred's apartment scene.

"What have I told you about getting up on that ladder?" Miss Carolyn asked, hands firmly on her hips, silver eyebrow firmly raised. Kate avoided her gaze. She focused instead on breaking down the ladder for storage, no easy task considering the ladder's height.

"Tomorrow's the big day and everything has to be perfect."

"There've got to be a thousand lights on that tree. How in Heaven's name did you spot the broken one?"

There were actually 12,460 lights on the Main Street Christmas tree, but Kate didn't want to correct her boss. Or look like the biggest festival nerd in town, though everyone probably already suspected as much. She shrugged.

"It's a gift."

To be fair, her eagle eye came more through experience than through some miracle of heavenly gift-giving. A lifetime of staring up at the tree with joy and awe had taught her the weak electrical spots. With the ladder broken down and folded, Kate scooped up the handle, groaning with the effort. She'd definitely feel the strain in her muscles tomorrow, but it was all worth it for that one tiny light. If the tree brought joy and the holiday spirit to even one person, Kate's mission would be accomplished. Christmas Eve was the night the crowds were the densest and most hopeful; Kate didn't want even one thing to go wrong for them.

She started off for Town Hall to return the ladder. With its balcony level and classic architecture, the main ballroom was used as Scrooge's house, but they used some of the anterooms and recreation rooms for storage and costume changes. Miss Carolyn followed behind.

"You're my best worker, kid, but you're stubborn as they come."

"We *make* Christmas for people, Miss Carolyn. What we do is important, right down to the tiniest little light bulb."

"You really love this, don't you?"

"More than anything."

Kate didn't need to think about that for more than a second. Her entire life revolved around the festival. As far as she was concerned, Christmas was the best time of year. Not because of the presents or the food, though those were certainly part of it. To her, Christmas was the one time of year when everyone put aside their differences and sat together at the table of humanity. Hope lit the lamps and compassion played the music. Christmas wasn't a holiday but a microcosm of the best of mankind, a reminder of what they could be if they only carried the spirit with them all year round.

It also made her excessively poetic.

"Well." Miss Carolyn cleared her throat and pulled Kate away from the side door. "I need you to come with me."

"Why?"

"We have a visitor from Woodward. And they're waiting on us."

The swinging of the heavy, oaken front doors of the town hall punctuated the ominous line. Heavy ladder still in tow, Kate stepped through the main marble atrium to see they were not entering some intimate meeting with their corporate overlords.

Judging from the sheer number of people present, the room looked more like an intervention than a meeting to discuss cost-cutting measures or whatever it was corporate decided to throw at them next.

Heads turned at the doors opening and a sea of worried, familiar faces turned to greet them. Mitch and Betsy Plinkett held hands and stared with distant eyes. Lindy Turnbull's perfect skin wrinkled with concerned lines. Even little Bradley Lewisham, their Tiny Tim, gripped his prop cane until his knuckles went white. Costumes mingled with plain clothes, but one thing was consistent: fear.

Something had happened. Or was happening. And no one had told Kate about it. Her stomach dropped too far for her to pick it back up. She glanced sidelong at Miss Carolyn. She was a rock of consistency and positivity. If there was a North Star in this room, she would be it.

But when Kate looked, there was no guiding light to follow. Miss Carolyn's rosy cheeks sunk into a pale shade of gray. Her eyes hardened. Dread prickled the hairs on the back of Kate's neck. If whatever happened was enough to rankle their leader, it could only mean one of two things. Either someone had died, or they were getting shut down.

"Good evening."

Kate's head snapped to the front of the room, where a hastily constructed podium and a microphone stood. Too distracted by her friends and neighbors, she hadn't noticed the setup when she walked in, but now it was all she could do to even blink. Behind the podium stood a solitary man. Against the white walls of the atrium, his black suit and golden hair stood out with the entrancing shock of an abstract painting, as if he were nothing more than lonely brushstrokes on a canvas.

He was also, as far as Kate could see, the only person in the room without an identifiable expression in his face. For someone so young—he couldn't have been more than a few years older than her, if that—he had the practiced look of a lifelong poker player. She wouldn't have stood a chance against him in a game of Hold 'Em. His natural state seemed to be one of stone. Worse still, when he spoke, she realized it wasn't just a skin-deep distinction. His unavailable emotions went all the way to his core.

"My name is Clark Woodward, and it's my sad duty to inform you that my uncle, Christopher Woodward, passed away last month."

Gasps from every corner of the room, including Kate's. Mr. Woodward was a good, kind man. He lived in Dallas, but he made time every month to come and visit the ranches in Miller's Point, and of course he visited the festival every year. He even played Scrooge in the festival once, after the real Scrooge took ill and couldn't get out of bed. What he lacked in acting skills, he made up for with the biggest heart in all of Texas. Kate cracked at the news, but the young man behind the podium held his hand up for quiet, effectively silencing them with a single gesture. He wasn't done yet.

"As the new CEO of my uncle's company, it is also my duty to inform you that we will be shutting down The Christmas Company subsidiary, effective immediately."

CEO. Uncle. Shutting down. Immediately. The words all made sense individually, but when sliced into that order and delivered with such dignity, Kate wasn't sure she understood them. How could *this* man be Mr. Woodward's nephew? Who made him CEO?

Kate didn't even flinch when her shaking hands dropped the folded ladder with a room-shaking *thunk*, drawing the attention of a room full of her friends and neighbors. The other questions and confusions were nothing in the face of her biggest issue.

Destroying The Christmas Company would mean

the end of Miller's Point as they knew it. Woodward's ranching operations made many of the families good livings, but the seasonal work meant working for The Christmas Company during the colder months was all that stood between many in Miller's Point and the stinging crush of poverty. Her chest tightened in pain at the reality of it.

Around her, the room erupted into conversation and denials, questions and protestations, each more vehement and heartbreaking than the last. But Kate remained squarely focused on their executioner as he dealt the final death blows, not caring if they could hear him over their distressed chatter.

"All salaried and hourly staff will receive a generous severance package, and I will remain in town for the next few weeks as I oversee the dissolution of the company. Any questions can be directed to the phone number found on your severance letters, which will be in the mail in the next five to seven days. We thank you for your years of service."

With the crowd still reeling from the announcement, he stepped down from the microphone and moved to leave the room. Just like that. Without any warning and without any apologies, he marched down the hall's middle aisle towards the front door. People watched him as he passed, still talking among themselves, but no one said or did anything to stop him, not even Kate. She watched his mirror-shine shoes take command of the floor as if he owned the land he walked on. *Step, step, step, step.* It beat the tune of a song no one wanted to sing, the song of finality. A song that ended with the slam of the chamber doors behind him.

When there was nothing left of him but the faint whisper of cold air, the assembled crowd turned back towards Miss Carolyn. Some of them surely caught Kate in the periphery of their gazes, but she, too, stared at the weathered old woman for some sort of comfort. Miss Carolyn always had a plan. She had a plan and contingency for every scenario. The hall was silent. Kate couldn't even hear her own breathing. Everyone waited for Miss Carolyn's wisdom to save them.

But when she didn't speak and instead turned to Kate with wide, wet eyes, the younger woman understood their wished-for wisdom would never come. The dread fluttering in Kate's stomach turned to lead as the reality of their situation fully sank in. If Miss Carolyn didn't know how to save them, they'd already lost.

"I," she began, her voice wavering from tears. The room seemed to lean in. Here it was. The big speech to rally the town and save Christmas. She opened her mouth once. Then twice. She scanned the room, meeting the expectant eyes gazing at her.

And then, just when everyone thought she'd give them all the answers, Miss Carolyn slumped. A wrinkled hand ran its way through her hair and she sighed deep enough and defeated enough for all of them combined. "I'm tired. I think I'm going home. Y'all should, too."

For a moment, no one obeyed. They waited for a

punchline, for a "just kidding. Let's go punch the big city rat until he gives us what's ours." She met their hope with nothing but silence. Slowly people stood and collected their things, muttering well wishes for the season to their friends and neighbors.

Kate didn't move. Every time she blinked, more of her life crumbled before her. There would be no Christmas Eve festival tomorrow night. There would be no Christmas celebration. Scrooge would never again sing. The town would never celebrate its nightly tree lighting ceremony again. Friendships forged over the festival would dissolve. Some families would lose their main livelihood, others their supplemental income and others still would lose a reason to stay alive through the winter. The charities they supported would go unfunded. The town might not even survive without the tourist income. Kate's found family would disintegrate, just like that. Everything was lost.

As the thought occurred to her, a little sniffle made itself known. It was so clear and so loud she couldn't ignore it. Kate turned to find little Bradley hiding his tears behind his Tiny Tim cane. Kate wondered briefly how many other children had worn that cap before him. How many lives had been changed by those children? What would those people have been without the festival?

Who would *she* be without the festival?

The questions were more convicting than the answers, and the brain-piercing goodbyes of her chosen family were one big key turning the ignition of her fury. This was her family. No one was going to tear it apart. Not as long as she had a say.

"Stay here, Miss Carolyn."

"Kate...what are you doing?"

Miss Carolyn's question wasn't going to stop her. Kate apparently no longer had a job to lose; she no longer had to listen. These people were her family, her community, and she wasn't going to stand by while some stick-in-the-mud Dallas boy tried to tear them apart and make this world a little bit worse.

With a spine as straight as a flagpole and chin held twice as high, she stormed out of the Miller's Point Town Hall. Her hammering heart joined the steady rap of her shoes as she jogged down the front steps towards the shadowed figure in the black sport coat.

"Hey!"

He was the only one on the street, hence the only one she possibly could have been talking to, but he didn't respond to her hail. The flames of frustration and anger licked at the back of her neck, threatening to consume her. She tried to keep them at bay and maintain some semblance of coolness—the last thing she wanted was to be accused of being an emotional or irrational woman by this stranger—but it was next to impossible. When she thought about all the lives this one tiny decision would touch, it burned up every sense of rational control she possessed.

"Hey, Woodward!"

Was it the use of his name, her razor-sharp tone or the whipping wind that caused him to tense up like that? Kate didn't care, as long as he paid attention to her. She closed the small space between them, catching up to him just in front of the Scrooge and Marley office. During the off-season, it served as a general store, but she called it the Money-House all year round. Not even the sight of it, which usually sent a thrill of sentimentality through her, could calm her now. When he didn't turn to face her, she took the liberty of hopping down off of the curb so she stood directly in his eye line. This forced her to gaze up at him, but she didn't think there was anything doe-eyed about her. If anything, she felt like an avenging Valkyrie, riding for justice. No one, not even this arrogant stranger, would make the mistake of underestimating her.

"What do you think you're doing?"

His face remained as composed and disinterested as ever, but Kate spied the fingers of his right fist clenching and unclenching. She almost smiled. He had a tell; something was bothering him.

"I'm looking for my car," he announced.

"Your car?"

"Yeah, I parked my car here," he pointed to an empty space in front of Town Hall, "earlier today and now it's gone. It's a rental."

"It got towed, then."

"Towed?"

"We don't allow cars in town during the festival. It ruins the illusion."

Kate almost laughed as she said it, but quelled the urge to do so by crossing her shivering arms over her chest. Everyone with half a brain knew no cars could come into town during the festival. It was on every brochure and article ever written about their little Christmas town; plus, the Martins made a tidy penny renting out their field as a parking lot during the winter. Yet another source of income they'd lose if this guy managed to go through with his plan.

"You should be thanking me, then. I'm modernizing the place already." His tone managed to be smug even as she wondered if the slight shrink of his shoulders meant he might not entirely believe that. "Who do I call about getting it back?"

What arrogance! She'd come out here to give him a piece of her mind and he had the audacity to ask her about his *car*?

"I don't think you're going anywhere until you give us some answers."

"With all due respect, I don't owe you answers."

"Oh, really?"

"For my years of service focusing on profitable divisions of his business, my uncle left me the company and I'm doing my best to protect his legacy."

"His legacy? Look around you! This is his legacy!"

She said *is* when she supposed she should have said *was*. Though, in Kate's estimation, a man's legacy didn't die with him; it was a living, growing thing that outlasted him and stretched as long as other people cultivated it. Mr. Woodward would only really die if they let this festival die with him. It was yet another reason Kate continued to fight, even when this arrogant jerk couldn't stop staring down the bridge of his nose at her like she was no more than a receipt stuck to the bottom of his shoes.

"This festival isn't profitable."

"Maybe not in money, but—"

"What other kind of profit is there?"

Kate opened her mouth and closed it twice, not because she didn't know the answer to his question, but because she knew it wouldn't move him. He was a numbers and cents guy. Telling him what the festival lost in funds it more than made up for in revival of the human spirit probably wasn't going to do anything other than make her out to be some silly, sentimental woman.

Which she was. But she just didn't want him thinking it.

"No?" he asked. If she were the fighting type, she might have punched that smug, condescending smirk of victory off of his face, but she refrained. "Yeah, that's what I thought. Now, tell me who I call about the car."

"I could." Rather than violence, Kate decided to deal in bitingly sweet sarcasm. "But I have to do what's best for my town, just like you have to do what's best for your company. And I don't think it's good for us to have a lunatic like you out on the road."

"If I hear you out, will you give me the number?"

She'd meant her quip about him driving around town as a joke, but he responded as though they were finally speaking the same language: the language of transaction. In some ways, Kate had to admire him for that. He was as single-minded in his determination as she was; they shared a sincere faith in the rightness of their cause. Sure, he couldn't have been more wrong, but at least he believed in something, even if it was just the power and importance of money. He shoved his hands in his pockets.

"I'll consider it."

"Then I'm listening, Miss...?"

"Kate."

"Kate."

It must have been a strong, random winter wind sending chills through her body; it couldn't have been the almost tender way he said her name. She coughed and tightened her arms across her chest, hoping the pressure would stop the sensation.

"What should I call you? Scrooge McDuck, or...?"

To her surprise, he laughed. It wasn't an evil movie villain laugh or anything, just a nice chuckle with a warm ring to it. She dismissed how much she liked it as a fluke. Even cold, unfeeling statues sometimes looked almost human in the right lighting.

"You can call me Clark."

Kate didn't repeat his name as he did hers. It somehow felt wrong to call him by his first name; she felt more comfortable calling her former high school teachers by their first names than she did calling him Clark. It was such a wholesome, all-American kind of name. Clark Kent. Clark Gable. Clark Woodward wasn't the correct third for that trio.

"Listen." All of Kate's strength went into fueling her empathy for this man. Focusing on her friends and family would just leave her angry and bitter; focusing on him would give her a much better shot. Most men liked an appeal to vanity. Maybe it would work on him. "I don't know you. I don't know anything about you. But your Uncle Christopher was a good man. He believed in this town. I mean, your family basically built this place. The library is named after you. The school auditorium. The football field. The gazebo in the park, for goodness' sake. It's all yours. You can do whatever you want with it—"

"Great. You understand where I'm coming from."

"No. I mean, yes, but you don't understand where I'm coming from." He raised an eyebrow, which she took as a sign to continue. "You have a town full of people who stare at your name every day with hope. And gratitude. Are you going to betray all of these people? Take away their livelihoods?"

"I don't know any of these people. I don't care about any of these people."

Those two statements landed on Kate's jaw like a string of one-two punches. What kind of man just… didn't care?

"If they want jobs, they can herd cattle like the rest of my employees, but I can't waste money on this Christmas foolishness for another day."

"But your uncle—"

"I am not my uncle!"

It was a roar, a statement to the heavens; the force

of it almost knocked Kate back a step. Somehow, she managed to hold her ground even as she couldn't quite understand the nerve she'd struck. Everyone wanted to be Mr. Woodward; he was as kind as he was insanely rich. The perfect combination. What kind of man hated a man like that?

"Clearly."

The sharp flash of emotion dissolved as quickly as it appeared. Clark straightened his jacket.

"I think I've heard enough. You can go ahead and give me that phone number now."

"One last thing," Kate said.

"Yes?"

"During your... During your little speech, you didn't even wish us a merry Christmas."

His refusal to do so left her with a nasty taste in her mouth. A small gesture it might have been, but its absence was so blatant she couldn't let it go.

"That's because I don't celebrate Christmas."

"Don't celebrate Christmas?" Kate choked.

"No. Now, give me the number."

Dumbstruck, Kate's brain didn't quite possess the processing power to say anything as she gave him the number. The cogs in her mind were too busy trying to puzzle out his declaration. But once he had the number, he was gone, leaving her with nothing but questions. There was no goodbye. No, "for what it's worth, I'm sorry." Just a curt "thanks," as he walked away dialing. Kate stood alone on the sidewalk for only the briefest of seconds before a hand touched her shoulder. She didn't turn around or tear her gaze from the spot where Clark stood just a moment ago; she knew who would be there.

"How'd it go, dear?"

The pity in Miss Carolyn's question stung. Kate hadn't even realized tears were forming in her eyes until they left cold tracks down her flushed cheeks. She'd failed. She'd tried to save her town, and she'd failed. With a weak shrug, she decided a little gallows humor was probably for the best.

"Do you know if any places are hiring?"

Chapter Two

Christmas Eve

Kate Buckner was on a roll, as far as rants went. Since arriving almost thirty minutes ago, she'd yammered nonstop, flooding her companion and the empty restaurant with her every stray thought. The faster she spoke, the faster they came, leaving her to race to catch up.

"But you know what I really can't stand?"

It was 7:15 on the morning of Christmas Eve, and for the first time since she was seven years old, Kate wasn't ironing a petticoat or setting up trays of mince pies. For once, she sat at the end of the bar at Mel's Diner, drinking a steaming cup of coffee and relishing the hearty scents of bacon and maple syrup. On a regular morning in, say, March, the old diner was the greatest breakfast joint in the known universe.

But this Christmastime? She hated it. Mel's was a staple of the Miller's Point diet and she came in here at least once a week, but that was part of the problem.

Without the festival, this felt like just another Tuesday. Bing Crosby's holiday standards on the old jukebox just weren't enough to convince her this was actually Christmas Eve.

"What can't you stand?"

Michael Newman, her breakfast companion and best friend since they were cast as Fred and Fred's wife in high school, couldn't have been more different than Clark Woodward. Where the out-of-towner played perpetual poker, Michael slapped himself open and let you read every page of him. He was the all-American type, dark-skinned with a smile that could light up a football stadium on its own, the exact image of a small-town golden boy. She'd always assumed he'd be mayor one day, but now she wasn't sure if the town would be around long enough for him to make the leap from ranch medic to political mastermind. For a long time, town gossip had it that the two of them, the town's two favorite children, would end up married, but she could never imagine it. They were like two trees planted too close together. Their branches intertwined and they shared the same soil, but they'd never become one. She only thought of him as a friend.

"What I *really* can't stand is that he has the audacity to stand there and mansplain to me about economics. Of course the festival doesn't make money for them, but it makes money for us, and that helps keep the town—the town where his business is, I'll remind you—afloat. What's he gonna do about workers when they all move to Fort Worth or something because there's not enough money circulating here? Huh?"

"I don't know, Kate."

The diner was completely empty, perhaps because it wasn't meant to be open. It closed on Christmas Eve and Christmas Day, usually because Mel, a rotund, redheaded man with a missing front tooth, always played The Ghost of Christmas Present, but this morning Kate had showed up at his front door with a determined knock and Michael in tow, ready to pay top dollar for black coffee and as many pancakes as it was humanly possible to consume in one sitting. She couldn't fathom sitting alone in her tiny apartment above the town's solitary bookstore for another minute, looking out onto the empty town square; the loneliness would have consumed her.

Now, all that consumed her was the frustration she'd been venting to herself all night. Saying these things out loud helped slightly, but as usual, Michael wasn't content to nod his head and agree with her. He just had to be difficult. The man never knew when to quit, an admirable quality he and Kate shared.

"And who doesn't celebrate Christmas? Christmas!" she exclaimed, waving her hands in her usual manner, the kind that almost always ended in her accidentally knocking over a salt shaker or a full glass of Diet Coke.

"Off the top of my head? Jewish people, Muslims, Jehovah's Witnesses, some other sects of Christianity, some atheists—"

The sass earned him a withering look.

"I don't know, Kate. Maybe he just doesn't like..." Michael picked at his biscuits and gravy, the first course of the six he'd ordered immediately upon sitting down at the bar. After half a lifetime of friendship, Kate had taught him these moods of hers meant he would need to be settled in for a long, long time. "I don't know. Trees. Maybe he's allergic to Christmas trees."

"He could get a fake one."

"Or he gets paper cuts from wrapping presents."

"He could use gift bags."

"What about eggnog? Maybe he's vegan."

"Then he needs to move out of Texas."

On some level, Kate knew she was being useless. Sitting in this diner complaining about the impossibility and injustice of it all seemed like a perfect way to get absolutely nothing done. On another level, the impossibility and injustice almost gave her permission to whine. Nothing could be done. Why shouldn't she just moan and groan and commiserate with her friend? She dropped her head into her hands.

"I don't want to be that guy," Michael said through a mouth full of biscuit, "but you don't look so good."

"I don't know why. I got a solid four hours of sleep last night. That's a full hour longer than usual."

Kate knew full well how she looked. Besides her daily uniform of jeans, a red flannel shirt, her reliable pair of sturdy-heeled boots and her dirty blonde hair tied away from her face in a sensible braid, heavy bags dragged her hazel eyes down and her splotchy skin spoke of a restless night. Michael was more of a solid eight hours of sleep kind of guy, so his surprise was understandable.

"What were you doing up that late?"

Kate brightened up. Her ideas may have been half-baked, but at least she had them. And even if it would never happen, she liked feeling useful.

"Brainstorming. I have tons of ideas to save the town." And only two of them involved hiring Bono and Beyoncé for a telethon. Most of the others involved social media campaigns and petitioning the federal government for a grant of some kind once she figured out how to write grants, but some of the ideas were sensible and others not cooked up. "We're gonna call the governor and petition to have the square designated a historical—"

Her ranting came to an abrupt halt as Michael's fork clattered to his plate and his jaw dropped halfway to the floor. He stared over her shoulder at something Kate couldn't see. She tried to make it out in the reflection of a window behind *his* head, to no avail.

"No way," he said.

"What?"

"Don't look now," he muttered, casually reaching for his coffee cup, "but your boyfriend from yesterday's meeting just walked in."

"My what?"

Kate spun in her seat, but Michael caught her shoulder and pulled her back to face front.

"I said don't look now!"

Thank goodness for the Bing Crosby Christmas

hits. If it hadn't been for the loud crooning, Clark Woodward would've heard them. Mind racing, Kate tried to place the pieces of this puzzle together. This was their town and their diner. He must have thought himself as bulletproof as the real Clark Kent if he thought he could show his face in public after what he did yesterday.

"Why is he here?" Kate hissed, leaning into Michael to prevent herself from giving in to the temptation to glance over her shoulder at the intruder.

"I don't know. He's just sitting at a table, looking at a menu."

"What in the world does he think he's doing? Is he going to shut this place down, too?"

"Maybe he's just hungry."

"No." Kate shook her head. He wasn't a diner breakfast kind of guy. He was a protein bar and kale smoothie kind of guy. Dallas men always gave off a clean living vibe; it made them unable to function in a small town like Miller's Point. "He's got to have something up his sleeve."

"Shh. Mel's going to take his order."

They fell into silence as Mel's heavy steps took him towards the booth behind Kate. She tuned her ears for any whisper of underhanded moneygrubbing. The first time Clark tried to barter over the price of eggs, she was going to flip.

"Hi, stranger." Mel greeted him with the same warmth and openness with which he greeted everyone. His friendliness crawled under Kate's skin. Clark didn't deserve Mel's good nature. He deserved a one-way ticket straight out of town. She believed in universal good. Everyone had wonder and joy inside them. Everyone could be reached with kindness. But...this guy made her so mad she could spit. "What can I get you?"

"Yeah, can I have a double stack of buttermilk pancakes and a black coffee to go? With a side of bacon, too."

Even with her back turned, Kate could picture him in her mind's eye, sitting unmoved with the perfect winter backdrop behind him. His voice was as flat and lifeless as she'd heard it. Still, she applauded his order. Simple, direct, and he even got some of Mel's famous double-crispy bacon. Maybe he was human after all.

"To go? You off somewhere?"

"Work."

"Work? It's Christmas Eve, kid. Didn't anyone tell you?" Mel chuckled. He always made conversation with his customers. Maybe it was a small-town gossip thing or maybe it was a Mel thing, but he liked keeping up to speed with the movement of his community.

"It's a Tuesday. I work on Tuesdays."

Apparently, Clark didn't appreciate the perceived intrusion.

"Ah. I see." There was a pause, awkward in its length. Kate picked at her own pancakes to give off the appearance of not eavesdropping. "It's just...I don't know if anyone's gonna be in the Woodward office this morning. Most people would have the day off for the festival. Besides, even if anyone is in, they won't be there until nine, at least."

"All because of Christmas?"

"Yeah. Christmas is kind of a thing around here."

Understatement of the century. Christmas was a way of life, and Clark couldn't even begin to understand how terribly he'd disturbed it. A pang of sympathy tugged at her. His cronies in Dallas almost certainly worked on Christmas Eve, the poor big city stiffs.

"I'll just have my breakfast here, then. Thanks."

"Don't you have a family or anything to visit? I know it's not any of my business, but you seem pretty young to be wasting your holiday in a boring office."

"You're right." Newspaper pages rustled. "It isn't any of your business."

"Buttermilk pancakes, bacon and coffee." Another awkward pause spread between them like butter on a biscuit, ending only with Mel tapping his pen against his tiny ordering notepad. "Coming right up."

The interaction ended with Mel whistling as he returned to the kitchen and Michael turning back to Kate with untamed shock. He probably expected to see steam coming out of Kate's ears. If anyone had told her she wouldn't be hopping mad at Clark for speaking to someone in her town that way, she would have laughed in their face. But her mind caught on something and unraveled like a home-knit sweater.

Don't you have a family?

It isn't any of your business.

For the first time since meeting him, the anger

and hurt serving as Kate's most recent and dear best friends were nowhere to be found. In their place stood a different creature altogether. She no longer hated the man threatening to take her life away.

She pitied him.

All of her assumptions about him had to be, on some level, incorrect. In her mind, she fancied him living the perfect, big-city rich boy life. A huge family who lavished him with gifts and privileges, love and understanding.

Yet, here he was. Alone. In a diner booth. On Christmas Eve. Waiting for his office to open so he could spend the day working.

How sad was that?

Kate's entire heart smashed open, and the blindness of her own rage smacked her in the face. Guilt bittered the coffee in her mouth, but it was soon replaced. Her eyes widened, she reached for Michael's hand, and let her hopes get as high as they pleased.

This was a solvable problem. Clark Woodward's loneliness was one hundred percent solvable.

"Can you distract him for a few hours?" she asked, knowing full well the monumental burden she'd shoved onto her friend's admittedly toned shoulders. Michael's eyes widened. As usual, he was an open book. Fear wrote itself on his every page.

"*What*?"

"I think I have a plan." Well, half a plan. Quarter of a plan. A fraction of a plan. She'd work out the rest on her bike. "Can you distract him until, like, noon?

And then bring him to the old Woodward place? I think that's where he's staying."

"You wanna leave me with that?"

Kate stood and threw on her layers of sweaters and scarves, all while her mind wrote plans and made to-do lists. When she was done, she gave him a firm pat on the back for good luck. She wouldn't want his job, either, but he was the only person she trusted with the task. No one said no to Michael. Even in a world with Tom Hanks, Michael took the top prize for most effortlessly likable guy on earth.

"You're the best guy in town. If you can't do it, no one can. I believe in you."

"But—! But—!"

His protests faded as she sprinted from the diner and hopped on her bike, which was waiting outside for her. As she pedaled towards the massive mansion on the far side of town, speeding past Dickensian facades and garlands, Kate's motives solidified. There was only one way to save Miller's Point. There was only one way to save the festival. There was only one way to save the solitary man in the diner from his own self-imposed darkness and isolation.

She had to make Clark Woodward believe in Christmas.

Chapter Three

It was so provincial. Clark Woodward couldn't think of any other word to describe Miller's Point. Provincial in every sense of the word. Nearly everything about them revealed how small they were, and what was worse, they reveled in their smallness. They clung to their superstitious belief in the holidays. They fought the inevitable march of progress he was going to bring to the company and their backwater enclave. The diner didn't even have avocado on the menu.

As he waited for his pancakes, Clark opened the newspaper. They didn't get the *Dallas Observer* out here, so the local gossip would have to do. He scanned the words, each one sinking in less deeply than the one before it. Out of the window framing his booth, he could see the entire town square, including the town hall, where only yesterday he and Kate—he never got her last name—had faced off.

Last night, he hadn't allowed himself the time or the thought to take in the beauty of the town's historic district. And it really was beautiful, even if it being beautiful just reminded him how wasteful the entire enterprise was. How much money did they spend on these facade recreations of London's Cheapside? How much of his family's fortune got washed away every night with those fake snow machines? And the lights! They might as well have built a fire out of all the greenbacks they wasted.

Wasteful and beautiful. The worst combination.

More dangerous, though, was thinking about the beauty who'd dared to challenge him. She'd burned herself into him yesterday with her persistence and the fiery passion behind her eyes.

He appreciated how strangely alike they were, even as they fought for completely different goals. If he hadn't been spooked by her insistence that his uncle would have saved the festival, he could have stayed on those steps and talked to her for hours. She was a sharp debater with a biting wit. In a town like this, he'd expected to be greeted as a king. His family, after all, was responsible for their survival. But she didn't bow and scrape; she challenged him.

She was wrong, of course, and he was right. But the challenge still thrilled him, even if he didn't dare let it show on his face. He didn't want anyone thinking they had any kind of power over him.

The most striking thing about her, perhaps, was her ability to embody everything he despised about Miller's Point. That dichotomy of wasteful and beautiful dwelled within her. She had much to offer;

he saw that even in their brief interaction. Yet, she chose to stay in Miller's Point, where she could do nothing but waste her life putting up tinsel.

Clark knew he should push all thoughts of her directly from his head. A distraction like her would only get in the way of his plans. His mission was simple, but like a fine watch, even the slightest bit of sand carried the potential to destroy everything. In three steps, he could be done with this stupid festival. Step One: Dissolve The Christmas Company. Two: Sell off its assets. Three: Return to civilization and Dallas before New Year's. He could only do that if all distractions were kept to a minimum and all pieces of sand stayed far out of his way.

And he could only accomplish his three-step plan if people actually went to work instead of spending their Tuesdays watching Hallmark movies or whatever it is they did when they "celebrated" Christmas. Clark's mind boggled at the way this town shut down on this useless holiday. The McDonald's, where he first attempted breakfast, had locked its doors.

"But—! But—!"

Clark's head popped up from the blurred words of his newspapers at the loud shouting of a stranger. He whipped his head around just in time to see a flash of a red-scarfed woman dash out of the door and a desperate man sitting at the diner counter. Clark was aware of small-town manners. A good citizen would have invited the freshly liberated man to join him for breakfast, but Clark wasn't a good citizen, and even if he was, he didn't think anyone in Miller's Point would particularly want to share a meal with him.

"Can you believe her?"

It took at least fifteen seconds for Clark to realize the other man was talking to him. He focused on an article about a high school track meet. Apparently, this small town dominated at the recent district meet, held at Christopher Woodward Stadium. He wondered if they'd keep the name now that his uncle was dead, or if they'd turn it into the Christopher Woodward Memorial Stadium to acknowledge his legacy or whatever.

"I wasn't listening. Sorry."

Apparently, to the man at the counter, this was all the invitation he needed to join Clark for breakfast.

"This seat taken?"

No, but it isn't open either. Please leave me and my pancakes in peace. Clark fought to keep the snark at bay. There was nothing he wanted less than company at the moment, especially when the entire town was afflicted with candy cane fever. He didn't want any of that foolishness rubbing off on him. But it didn't seem this guy was in the mood to take no for an answer.

"Go ahead."

"Thanks."

Balancing his array of half-finished plates across his forearms, he plopped into the seat, rattling the table. It took longer than a polite minute for the man to arrange his extensive breakfast, which only added to the heat flaring up the back of Clark's neck. His lips flattened into a thin line of displeasure when Mel appeared with a piping hot plate and mug. He placed them on the table, and Clark pulled them close, grateful for the distraction. He couldn't decide what the stranger across from him wanted, but if he thought he could convince him to change his mind about the festival, he'd be just as disappointed as Kate. Did these people have some sort of committee, dedicated to twisting the simplest of business decisions into a city-wide ordeal?

"One order of pancakes and bacon. And a black coffee. Syrup's over there. Can I get you anything else?"

Clark started to say no, but was cut off.

"Can I get some more coffee, Mel? Oh, and one of those blueberry muffins."

"They're about two days old."

"Can you pop it in the microwave for about thirty seconds, then?"

His easy intimacy with the diner owner put Clark's transactional replies to shame. Without the protection of his newspaper, Clark had to actually interact with these people. His worst fears realized.

"You got it, kid."

Mel departed. As Clark dug into his pancakes, he hoped the only frustration he'd have to deal with was the treacle-sweet music pouring out of the juke box, but his new guest proved him wrong.

"You're that Woodward guy, aren't you?" he asked through a mouth of biscuits dripping with gravy.

"Clark."

"I'm Michael." Clark nodded once, an acknowledgment that he'd heard the introduction, but his new companion took his silence as an invitation for more conversation. "Some people call me Buddy, but I'll answer to anything, really."

The urge to roll his eyes was unbearably strong. He couldn't imagine anyone wanting to be called Buddy when Michael was perfectly suitable. Buddy wasn't a name for a man. It was a name for a puppy or a background character in a Flannery O'Connor novel.

"Small towns," he muttered.

"Buddy was my grandfather's callsign during the invasion of Normandy. He won a Medal of Valor."

Clark choked on his bacon, ready to splutter out some kind of tense take-back of the insult, but he was awarded with uproarious laughter from the man across the table.

"I'm just messing with you, Dallas. Buddy used to be my nickname, but getting a medical degree changes how people see you. I mostly just go by Michael now. How're the pancakes?"

"Good."

"Mel makes the best pancakes in the whole state, I think. On Christmas morning, he sets up an assembly line in the town hall and a bunch of volunteers chip in to help him make, like, two thousand pancakes so everyone in town can have breakfast before the festival starts. The 25th is our busiest day of the year." Michael's hurried excitement tapered off when he realized a tradition would be ending. He got a hollow look in his eyes, which Clark did his best to ignore. "I mean, he did. And it was. When the festival was still on."

The festival. He was tired of hearing about the festival. If these people loved the festival so much, why didn't they put it on themselves instead of using his family's money? Better yet, why didn't they raise the price from a measly ten dollars per person to twenty-five per person? A fifteen-dollar increase would've meant big things for their bottom line, yet when he'd proposed it to Carolyn, the Director of Operations, she'd assured him she'd rather quit the whole thing altogether than keep poor families out and only cater to rich folks. She then glared at him as if the mere suggestion of raising ticket prices cheapened the entire heart of her operation.

Clark said, "Listen, Michael. I'm not really looking for company. I'm fine on my own."

"Yeah. Of course. I was just thinking I could maybe show you around, you know, give you the lay of the land since you'll be here for a few days. I can show you everything. Library, bank, even the parking lots so your car doesn't get towed again."

News travels fast. He'd only told Kate and the tow truck guy about his car; twelve hours later, everyone knew. *If I walk around with you for twenty minutes, will you leave me alone?* Something in this town's water must have made them especially persistent. As with his first interaction with Kate, Clark saw no other way to get rid of this guy than giving him a little bit of his time.

"Sure," he agreed, trying to hide his displeasure behind a half-hearted smile, only to be practically blinded by Michael's blinding one.

"Mel! Make my muffin to go!"

What Clark hoped would be a brief twenty-minute introduction became an almost three-hour walking tour of the most important historical and contemporary sites Miller's Point had to offer. By the time Michael ran out of steam, Clark knew more about the remote ranching village than he'd ever known about Dallas. For example, he'd had no idea his family founded Miller's Point outright. He assumed they'd settled and prospered here, not set up the first encampments of ranchers.

At the first half-hour mark of the extensive tour, Clark considered bailing out and begging off to his office, but he couldn't actually find it in himself to do it. Save for the workers taking down the decorations in the town square (as he'd instructed the night before), the town was empty and Michael was every bit the enjoyable host. Not that he ever let on, but he actually had a good time walking around the town and taking in its sights, provincial though they were.

But he drew the line at a cemetery tour. Close inspections of ghosts and tombstones where Jesus wore cowboy boots did not fit his description of an acceptable way to spend a morning. He checked his watch.

"I have to go to my office. I have things to do," he said, curt and direct as possible. The tour may have been a fine diversion for a few hours, but it couldn't last all day. He needed to be in the office, taking care of work, even if no one in this town seemed to understand the concept.

"Great! I'll walk you there."

"I'm fine, thanks—"

"No buts! Besides, I know where they hide the spare key."

The Woodward Building was two blocks east off of the town square, and unlike the Dallas offices, it was not an imposing block of concrete and steel, made up in an intricate Art Deco style. It was a humble, two-story building with a flat roof and little else to speak of besides the embarrassment of Christmas lights decorating the front windows. A hand-painted sign with flippable numbers read: "0 DAYS 'TIL CHRISTMAS." Clark ripped it from its hook as Michael went for the spare key.

"You really aren't into this Christmas stuff, are you?"

Given he'd only known this guy for a few hours, Clark spared him the tragic backstory and instead took the key and let himself in. The building's exterior appeared humble, befitting a small-town center of business operations, but the inside ruined his every hope of a muted, respectable workplace environment. It was too fancy. Though years of red-clay-covered boots marked and stained the carpet, the wood finishes of the desks and the crown molding belonged in a palace rather than a satellite office building. Christmas decorations, no doubt charged to his family's accounts, cluttered every available space. Even the coffee machine was top-of-the-line, but something else bothered him more. He made a beeline for the wall beside the receptionist's desk.

"What are you doing?" Michael asked.

"Turning the heating off," Clark replied, searching for the temperature gauge instead of asking what in the world he was doing standing around here when Clark had made it clear their little tour had ended at the graveyard gates.

"It's, like, forty degrees outside."

"And we all carry coats, don't we? Heating is expensive."

The other man's shocked gaze bore into Clark's skin. He paid it no mind. He was a practical man in every sense of the word; he didn't indulge in luxury. He wore fashionable but reasonably priced clothes, even stitching buttons and cuffs himself when they showed signs of wear. He wore his father's timeless suit jackets, having them tailored to fit perfectly. He wasn't very well going to heat an entire building, especially when no one worked inside to enjoy it. Besides, chill increased productivity. Hundreds of workplace studies said so. He'd stopped heating the office in Dallas;

everyone here would get used to it. His next order of business, while Michael underscored his movements with a warbling whistle version of "Baby, It's Cold Outside," was to find the receptionist's black book. When he finally procured it, he flipped through the pages, holding them close enough to his face to read them. He'd forgotten his glasses back at home.

"What're you doing now?"

"Calling my staff. *I* didn't give them the day off."

"You really think that's a good idea?" he asked. His boldness lasted up until Clark shot him a narrowed look over the secretary's desk. "It's just... They made plans. Want to see their families, you know."

"Why are you here? Why aren't you at work, I mean?"

"The foreman gave us the day off. We were all supposed to be out working on the festival to help with the Christmas Eve crowds. The 24th and 25th are packed. You wouldn't believe it."

"You work for Woodward?"

"Yep. On Ranch 13 on the Eastern lot."

Clark raised an eyebrow and flipped to another page in the contact book. No wonder the company suffered so much during the month of December. All of his employees were getting free passes from his foremen. If he had any say, everyone would be coming in to work this afternoon.

"I'll have to call him, too."

Passing pages upon pages of personal numbers and shoved-in food delivery menus, Clark finally reached the work associates section of the records and searched for his Head of Production's number. Whoever he was, he'd be getting an earful. Anyone who wanted to keep their job would be coming in, and that was final. Everyone in the Dallas office was working; there was no reason anyone else should have the day off. His fingers flew over the expensive black phone—only to receive the dial tone as Michael pressed down on the termination button. His eyes flashed with fear. Fear of what? Of hard work? This guy, with his big, calloused hands, didn't seem unaccustomed to hard work.

"Listen, I have to tell you something."

"...Yes?"

Returning the phone to its cradle, Clark waited for his companion to speak. Michael checked his watch, a gesture Clark couldn't help but note. Their tour had lasted an eternity without Michael checking his watch once; now he read the thing like the Gospel. The entire air hummed with nervous panic, though Clark couldn't for the life of him understand what Michael had to be nervous about. Surely the company's employees weren't this afraid of a hard day's work...right? Or did they really fear losing their precious day off so much?

"You know Kate Buckner?"

It wasn't the question he'd expected. Perhaps he should have. She'd been hovering in his thoughts like heavy-handed foreshadowing all day. He filtered her in his mind like sea water, never quite seeing her clearly.

"I've met *a* Kate," Clark offered. The taste in his mouth soured and he offered a silent prayer that

Michael's sudden declaration did not concern the Kate who cornered him outside of Town Hall last night. *Dear God, let him be talking about a different Kate. Please.* If this strange small town had taught him anything so far, it was this: no one wanted to tangle with her.

"Pretty? Dirty blonde hair? Looks like she always wants to dance or fight?"

Clark wouldn't have put it that way. She never looked to him like a dancer or a fighter, though she carried herself with the natural grace of either. If he put any amount of real thought into her, he might have described her as a helper. She looked ready to help anyone and anything who needed her, even if helping meant she had to fight. It was an endearing quality; he would have admired it if he didn't think it was against her best interest.

"Yeah. I've met Kate Buckner."

"She's up to something." Michael spoke, gaining momentum with every word like a freight train. "She's at your family's house right now. I wasn't supposed to tell you, and I don't really know what's going on, but I think it's important you go home right now and check it out."

Truth be told, Clark hated that old place. He'd tried to avoid staying there the night before, but every hotel or bed and breakfast he approached informed him, polite as could be, they had no vacancy, so he'd bitten the bullet and returned to the mansion's creaking halls, choosing to sleep on a couch in the front living room to avoid diving too deep into the body of the house. He hadn't been there since he was a kid, and the memories wrapped around him heavier than the musty old blanket he'd slept under.

"The Woodward House?"

"Yeah."

He dreaded returning in the daylight, but he knew he had no choice. He didn't know her plan, but he couldn't let any harm come to the estate. The sham castle built on a hill still held the spirits of his family, and they required protection.

It was all he had left of his parents.

Collecting his coat, he tossed Michael the keys to his rental car, which he'd rescued from the tow yard this morning.

"Drive me there."

Chapter Four

"This all looks amazing! Can we move those candlesticks to the end of the hall? Oh, be careful with those ornaments! Just put the boxes down in the living room. We'll decorate the tree later."

Kate wasn't one to toot her own horn, but even she had to admit it: the Woodward House looked amazing. It wasn't all her doing, of course. She merely lugged a few boxes and used her copy of the house keys to let everyone inside. When she called Miss Carolyn to tell her of her plan, The Christmas Company phone tree went into full effect, and within an hour, most of the town's decorations were torn down from their places off of the square and almost one hundred people showed up at the Woodward House to ready it for Christmas. Thankfully, this place wasn't unfamiliar to the people of Miller's Point. Mr. Woodward had let them use it as a muster point for the festival for years, so once inside, everyone had a good idea of which archways and bannisters needed the most Christmas-ification.

It was a painfully simple plan, really, and everyone hopped on board quicker than she anticipated. All she had to do was teach Clark Woodward to love Christmas. The process of that began with a Christmas makeover of his house. After seeing his pitiful slump at Mel's diner, she took to imagining quiet, lonely Decembers passing by him in a dark apartment in Dallas, complete with Hungry Man dinners and falling asleep on the couch. The sort of Christmas she only imagined in her nightmares. It was clear he'd fallen out of love with Christmas—Kate didn't believe anyone naturally disliked the holiday—because it'd been too long since he'd had a wonderful one. She was going to reintroduce magic into his life, and by tomorrow morning when she was done with him, he'd have to agree to putting the festival back on.

It would be difficult, but she had an ace up her sleeve. Some people claimed it was impossible to change someone's heart overnight, but Kate knew better. After all, she'd read Dickens.

"I think we're all done inside. They're finishing outside, but do you want to light 'er up in here?"

"Yes! Just one second…"

Kate sprinted for the top of the grand staircase, her muscles tingling. Everything had to be perfect, and this was the moment of truth. She nodded to Billy Golden, the load-in specialist for the festival, who'd been running point for her since his arrival that morning. He stood at the foot of the stairs with an electrical dial in hand, waiting for her signal. She held up her hands, as if preparing to conduct a symphony. "Okay. Now."

Kate blinked, fully expecting that in the split second of her eyes being closed, she would open them to find herself completely immersed in the winter wonderland of her own creation.

"What have you done?!"

Oh, no. The voice of her target echoed through the grand foyer of the Eastlake Victorian-style manor, shaking the paintings on the walls and knocking crystals of the chandelier. All movement—including Kate's heart—halted. Her eyes lowered, step-by-step down the carpeted, garland-strewn staircase, until she reached the tips of his mirror-shined shoes. She recognized his voice even without peeking at his face.

There was no noise but the driving, tinkling melody of "We Wish You a Merry Christmas." It wafted through the house like the smell of fresh-from-the-oven gingerbread cookies.

Apparently, Clark Woodward didn't appreciate music or delicious gingerbread because he let out another yawp of displeasure:

"And turn that music off!"

Without so much as peeking up from his shoes, Kate touched the pause button on the phone in her pocket, effectively silencing her Bluetooth playlist.

Once, when she was a kid, Kate had gotten caught trying on the Ebenezer Scrooge costume, fake beard and all. The man playing the miser that year had a lisp and a bit of a limp, so she was dragging her left foot around the dressing room saying, "Merry *Chrithhhmathh*." To her everlasting shame and regret, he'd walked in on her mid-private performance.

She felt nearly as captured now.

Michael. She cursed his name. He was supposed to keep him busy until noon at least! Everyone was supposed to be safely back home so there would be no way of restoring the house to normal order. That was the entire point of the distraction. If Clark demanded his house be emptied of all Christmas cheer, the plan would be ruined.

You've got to do something, Kate's rational brain told her petrified tongue. *You can't just stand here like an idiot. It's starting to get awkward.* Hands shaking in her pockets, she wondered if she hadn't made a poor decision or two this morning. Not about the choice of an angel as a tree topper instead of a star—she stood by that. She wondered if she'd made a mistake in coming here at all. Was she beaten before she'd even started? Was she even strong enough to save her town? Why did she think she, the town's resident hem-stitcher and pie-placer, would be good or strong enough to defend them against disaster?

Kate straightened. It didn't matter if she wasn't strong enough. *He* didn't know she wasn't strong enough, and she could use that to her advantage. Besides, she had every right to be here. She picked her head up, adopting an impenetrable armor of optimism. This was Christmas Eve. These people were her family and friends. She *had* to save them all.

And she didn't know how to walk away from someone with eyes as cold as his. She'd just have to save him, too.

"Clark! How are you?"

Her smile sent him back a step. He must have expected her to whimper and scrape at his booming shouts. Good. She'd caught him off guard already. Once he'd recovered, he walked deeper into the foyer.

"What have you done to my house?"

"Your house? Does it have your name on it?"

Michael helpfully stepped forward.

"It does, actually. It's on the sign right out front."

"Don't you have a clock to check somewhere?" she snarked, sending him scurrying out of the front door, right behind Billy Golden.

With Kate at the top of the stairs and Clark at the bottom, she reveled in the literal high ground. All she had to do was hold onto it. She glanced out of the house's wide front windows. Though the decorations on the inside of the house were almost entirely complete, a near army of workers on ladders were still hard at work hanging lights outside.

"So." She placed a steadying hand on the top of the staircase banister, hoping it looked more like a power move than something necessary to keep her upright. "What do you think?"

"What have you done?"

"Is there an echo in here?" The quip, in her opinion, was brilliant, but he either didn't get the joke or purposefully withheld his laughter. Rude.

She gripped the banister tighter and gave a sweep of the grand atrium with her free hand. The chandelier hanging in the high, vaulted ceiling had been dotted with poinsettia plants and evergreens, giving the room a sweet, rich smell. Kate was glad for their perfume; it meant she couldn't smell the smoke coming out of Clark's ears. She would've been lying, though, if she didn't secretly derive pleasure from his displeasure. He'd made everyone she knew uncomfortable when he ended their employment yesterday. Maybe he deserved to be uncomfortable, too, even if she was trying to heal what she suspected was his broken, used-up heart. "We decorated for Christmas. Do you like it?"

Don't shout. Don't raise your voice. Don't even let her know this is bothering you. Just be clear, direct, and get the job done. Clark's internal pep talk was strong, but not strong enough to hold his bewildered frustration at bay. He flexed his right hand, a nervous habit he'd spent almost his entire life unsuccessfully struggling to break, and tried to answer her question. Did he like it?

"I'd like it to be taken down."

"I'm sorry. No can do."

She stood at the top of the staircase like some silent film star, taking control of the garish scenery. He didn't need to look around him to see the marks of her handiwork everywhere. His family's house—that cold monument to excess and emptiness—had been transformed. In his memory, this place was always closer to Wayne Manor than Hogwarts—a shadowy prison for cobwebs and abandoned family photos.

When he'd driven up with Michael this morning, however, he'd almost turned around, convinced they'd made a wrong turn somewhere. Woodward today looked nothing like it did in his dark memories. With every turn of his car's wheels, they moved closer and closer to a postcard of a Victorian Christmas, not the palace of pity he'd always known the place to be. Though men and women still busied themselves on high ladders arranging wreaths upon third-story windows and hanging lights along the roof, the picture was clear.

Matters only worsened when he arrived inside to see a house overflowing with decorations and frippery. (Yeah, frippery. He was so enraged he'd had to dip into his grandfather's vocabulary for a word to describe it.) Fresh, fragrant greenery and cardinal-red ribbons brightened the sallow walls. Fake icicles hanging from the doorways danced in the heated breeze and caught the abundant light. A train—an honest-to-goodness train set—ran circles around the fir standing sentry in the open living room, sending out real puffs of steam from its working engine. And, if he wasn't going crazy—which, to be fair, wasn't entirely out of the realm of possibility—he could've sworn he smelled gingerbread baking somewhere.

The whole thing was enough to make him puke chestnuts.

"Take it down," he growled.

He could only hope the backdrop of tinsel and baubles didn't undercut the weight of his infuriated stare. This was his house. His family's house. And she had absolutely no business being in here, much less taking the whole place over for her personal art project.

"I can't." She shrugged and began a descent down the stairs, her high-heeled boots making authoritative thuds with her every step. "Not by myself, anyway."

Beyond the closed front door, a series of engines turned over and sputtered to life. Clark's stomach sunk.

"Let me guess…"

"Everyone's already leaving. They've got to go home for Christmas Eve. There's no way I could take all of this down by myself. It'll just have to stay up."

She landed on the step above him, and their body language echoed their last encounter. Back then, she was below him, asking for something she had to know he couldn't possibly give. Now, he was the one at a disadvantage.

Taking stock of himself, Clark tried to catalogue his feelings. In business, these sorts of exercises kept him from flying off the handle during negotiations. He treated his emotions like items on an inventory list. They first needed to be counted, weighed, measured, and then neatly put away to keep from overwhelming him. It would have been easy enough if her caramel-candy eyes weren't so distracting. The color was extraordinary, but it wasn't their beauty he kept tripping over. It was her unguarded warmth he couldn't quite wrap his head around. What gave her the right to treat him like an old friend, welcome to open the doors of her heart and make himself at home inside? Hadn't she ever been hurt before? Clark managed to put those thoughts away before he asked any of those questions out loud, opting to reach for the glass icicles over his head.

"Fine. I'll take it down," he said.

"And risk breaking everything before you can sell it?" Clark's expression and stiff arms must have given him away. She adopted an air of false modesty. "Am I wrong? I thought you wanted to make money off of this once you dissolve the company."

"It belongs to me." He returned his hands to his pockets. The icicles would have to wait. He didn't know the first thing about storing all of this holiday garbage, and no one would buy bits of shattered glass. "Why shouldn't I sell it?"

"Of course you should." A breeze of sarcasm blew behind her as she stepped down from the staircase and headed straight for the living room. He followed close behind, not wanting her to break or put her Jack Frost spell over anything else in this house. "But I'm afraid you'll have to wait until Christmas is over. The icicles are here to stay. Besides, you respect a contract, right?"

"A contract?"

"In your uncle's contract with the city, he stipulates that this home can be used as a muster point for all festival-related activities. I have every legal right to be here."

Uncle Christopher...why would you do this to me?

"Why are you doing this? What do you want?"

"Let me put it to you this way: the festival was my home. It's been my home every Christmas since I was seven years old. You took my home away, so I think it's only fair I get to take yours." The living room had received as much treatment as the rest of the house, plus it contained the *pièce de résistance*. The Christmas tree. Clark seemed to remember the ceilings in this house being fourteen feet high, which meant the undecorated fir was thirteen and a half feet tall. At least. The glistening angel almost brushed the ceiling. "Don't worry. I'll be out of your hair once the season's over."

Clark tightened his jaw to keep it from dropping to the floor. She couldn't possibly mean what he thought she meant, especially not with the nonchalant way she swanned around the room, adjusting the nutcrackers on the mantel as if she hadn't just invited herself over for Christmas.

"What do you mean?"

"I mean you're stuck with me."

The decorations, he could handle. He'd just sleep in his car the next two nights and wake up to the world returned to normal on Boxing Day. A strange woman with an affinity for decking the halls? He wouldn't and couldn't allow it.

"Oh, no. You're not staying, too."

"Of course I am. I bought us matching PJs and everything."

He didn't want to know if that was true. Picking up her jacket and duffle bag, he started to shove all evidence of her inside. The scented candles waiting to be lit, the pile of inventory papers tucked away on an end table... It all had to go.

"I don't want you here."

"I'm also non-negotiable. Contract says so. I'm the foreman."

"You *can't* stay here."

"Why not?" she scoffed, pulling the duffel out of his hands and returning it to its place in the corner of the room. "Don't you have a guest room or twelve?"

"Because you can't, all right? You just can't."

The last thing Clark was inclined to do was examine her question. *Why can't I stay here?* The question was more thorny than she probably gave it credit for, and he wouldn't prick himself on the brambles just to satisfy her curiosity.

"What? You're going to kick me out in the snow?"

"It's not snowing."

She clucked, leaning back on the couch, as comfortable and at ease as if she were in her own house.

"I wouldn't be too sure about that."

He didn't know what possessed him. His rational mind knew it wasn't snowing. Better still, he knew it couldn't be snowing. In Texas, even as far north as they were, the worst they usually got was the occasional cold wind, frosty pond, or hypothermic cow. Yet, his raging heart shoved him towards the window, where he threw open the curtains to reveal that, indeed, not only had the entire front yard of his home been covered in a thick layer of snow, but there was a gentle snowdrift passing by the window.

In a small, private humiliation, Clark's breath caught at the sight. Then, he remembered himself. Snow in Texas wasn't beautiful. It couldn't be beautiful because it wasn't real. He remembered the town square, which had been similarly covered in a layer of snow so thick and so realistic he'd almost reached out to touch it, and his awe dissolved.

"Fake snow?"

"It's not a Dickens Christmas without snow. Lots of it."

"I wouldn't know." He slammed the curtains shut, a gesture which resulted in little more than an impotent swaying of fabric. "I've never read it."

Back turned, he couldn't see the shock play on her face, but he did hear the genuine gasp of surprise she let out at this declaration. He shouldn't have expected any less from this Christmas freak.

"Never read *A Christmas Carol*? Well, thank goodness you're letting me stay." He turned in time to see her rustling about in her bag, determination written on her soft features, but even the softest, sweetest, most determined face in the world couldn't deter him. "I think I've got my copy in here somewhere."

"I'm not letting you stay. You're leaving." He scooped up her jacket and offered it to her. "And now."

"But think about it: do you really want to be alone in this big house on Christmas?"

"Yes!"

It came out as more of an emotionally charged, beastly roar than he anticipated, but if his own shaking voice shocked him, it was nothing compared to the surprise he felt as Kate's defensive charm softened into sweet sacrifice. Her smile morphed from practiced composition into something altogether more compassionate, tender.

She no longer armed herself or wielded her warmth as a weapon. She held it up as a peace offering. Peace with this woman scared Clark even more than the thought of battling with her.

"I'm not letting you. No one should be alone during the holidays."

He reached for his cell.

"I'm calling the police."

"Great idea. You can tell Chief Stan and Officer Harris I said Merry Christmas. I think they're on duty until midnight, then the Fitts siblings take over."

This woman was just crazy enough about Christmas to wish *anyone* a happy day, even the men he called to arrest her, but this wasn't a genuine request. She was reminding him where the loyalties of this town actually lay, and it certainly wasn't with the man who was going to end the town's most important festival. The police probably weren't going to be on his side, especially not if they saw Kate as their champion.

Besides, his uncle had signed that contract.

"You're not going to leave, are you?"

"I'm not a monster. I'm not trying to steal your house or anything. I'll leave after I have my perfect Christmas." Kate pointed to the kitchen, which was connected to the living room by a swinging servant's door. Clark was sure now he smelled fresh gingerbread cookies. "Can I get you some eggnog?"

"I don't want eggnog. I want you to put everything back to normal."

Clark examined his options—the few he had. The decorations and the woman were fixtures here, at least for another few days. So, he saw only two courses of action. He could leave. Or he could stay.

"You're in Miller's Point for Christmas, Clark," she said, not unkindly. "This is normal."

He'd have to stay. He didn't have to stay in *this room*, but he would have to stay. Cutting his losses, Clark walked for the door. He'd just go upstairs and find an office to work in. Normal in Miller's Point... What, all smiles and well-wishes and cartoon red-nosed reindeer?

"Yeah. That's what I'm afraid of."

Chapter Five

Yeah, *that's what I'm afraid of.* He left her with that declaration, and all she could think was: *Well, at least I know you can feel something.*

No. The thought put him in an unfair light. He'd shown tiny flashes of emotions over the course of their two conversations. Rage. Annoyance. Frustration. Fear.

But the deep, aching loneliness she saw in him when she suggested he didn't have to spend Christmas alone resonated inside of her. Until now, this entire… spectacle was little more than a means to an end. She assumed he had to be, at least on some level, a lonely man. Does a content, happy, and fulfilled person *hate* Christmas? No. But she now realized her actions here could serve more than one purpose. She could help him and save the town. She could teach him the true meaning of Christmas while also restoring Christmas for the people she loved most in the entire world.

Despite what countless TV shows and movies had taught her, she really *could* have it all.

First, she needed to get him to come back into the living room with her. She knew that wouldn't happen just on its own. Shouting at him from the living room to come back and hang out with her so she could show him the beauty of the season probably wasn't her *best* bet.

"Think, Kate," she muttered to herself, pacing the living room. "Think."

Pacing the Persian rug, she surveyed the room. It was, in every sense of the word, rich. The house was built in a faux-Victorian style, an American collection of half-British angles and ornamentation, and the inside reflected Mr. Woodward's inclination to show off his wealth. He presented himself as a gaudy man, to say the least, and he never shied away from spending money or talking about spending money—a trait he clearly didn't share with his nephew. Kate's pacing only halted when she heard the movement of a loose tile in the kitchen.

"He's gone," she called. "You can come out now."

No sooner had she spoken than Michael burst from behind the swinging door, which smacked against the nearest wall. He huffed and puffed with the dramatics of an amateur opera singer, as if he'd been shoved into a tiny, airless closet instead of the well-stocked kitchen for the last ten minutes.

"What was *that*?" he spluttered, pointing at a random place in the room. Kate could only assume he meant to point at somewhere Clark stood, but she had no way of knowing for sure. It was obvious he'd been eavesdropping. She returned to her pacing, rolling over everything she'd learned about the man from their last encounter.

He was so cold. Not just in the way he spoke to her or saw the world, but in his eyes. He was frozen down to his heart. She just hoped a good Christmas fire could be lit and melt the ice and frost away, not just for their sake, but for his.

"*That*," she answered, a bit too smug for her own good, "was the first stage of my plan."

"And you just let him go?"

"Yeah." She ran a hand through her hair and checked her wrist for a ponytail holder she already knew wasn't there. Her dirty blonde hair was so long and thick it often broke the thin elastics, leaving her to fuss and fiddle with her locks whenever she got too nervous to think straight. Tugging on one strand of hair, as if to pull some wisdom from her own brain, she tried to lay down her plan. "He needs time to cool off. Nothing was going to get done by needling him."

"What's your genius plan now, huh?"

Genius. That was it. When she was seven years old, Miss Cartwright—owner of the music and dance studio near the center of town—told her she could be a genius piano player if she ever put her mind to it. When The Christmas Company said it would pay for her lessons if she used her skills for the festival every year, she'd readily accepted.

And as it happened, the Woodward House's living room housed the town's most beautiful and most expensive piano, which sat in the corner across from the Christmas tree, waiting to be played.

Kate wandered over to the ancient Steinway. Her fingers only just brushed the ebony cover. It shot a thrill through her, like touching a holy relic; she needed to approach with reverence.

"We're going to smoke him out of his room."

"How?" Michael asked, as she lifted the cover and took her place on the bench. Shaking his head, he immediately began a muttered stream of vain prayers. "Don't say with song. Please don't say with song."

Her fingers touched the keys. Out of tune. She winced, but pressed forward.

"With song," she confirmed.

It was perfect, really. So much had already been written and spoken about the power of music that Kate didn't think twice about this stage of her plan. Music spoke to the soul in a language unwhispered by any other tongue. Her screaming after him about the magic of the season wouldn't work, but her joyful voice raised in song might be enough to coax him out of his hiding place, wherever that might have been.

Michael didn't share her optimism.

"We're doomed. We're totally doomed. This isn't a song and dance kind of guy, Kate."

"I know." She cracked her knuckles. It was going to take a lot of singing to cover the flaws of this piano's lack of tuning, but she never backed away from a challenge.

Besides, she listed "singing Christmas carols" as one of the Special Skills on her resumé. Without knowing it, she'd trained for this exact moment her entire life. "That's why this is going to work."

"And what's your plan after this, hmm? Make him fall in love with you and the town, like in one of those movies you love so much?"

"I'm *not* going to fall in love with Clark."

"Right. Because you're going to be an old maid and Miller's Point and the festival will be your family and your children. I've heard this speech before. Besides, I didn't say anything about *you* falling in love with *him*. I said *he* would fall in love with *you*."

"Love doesn't factor into this plan at all," she rushed out, eager to be done with this particular conversation. Whenever she and Michael broached the topic of her love life, they played out the same old song and dance. She reminded him that romantic, all-consuming, life-changing love never entered her mind as a possibility for herself. The pickings in town were slim and most of the people they went to high school with were paired off by the summer after senior year. And even if some handsome stranger did ride into town and she did want to fall in love with him, she wasn't even sure she knew how to go about doing it.

And then, he'd remind her that anyone could fall in love—no one *knew* how to fall in love; it just happened—and they'd go around and around in circles. She didn't have time for circles and talk of romance today, especially not in the context of Clark

Woodward. "We're going to do Christmas our way. And…" Her fingers ran along the keys, testing them out one by one in no particular order. She struggled to articulate her thoughts. "He's got this thing about him. He's lonely. I can tell."

"He's inherited a corporation worth millions of dollars, at least. I think he cuddles a body pillow stuffed with hundred-dollar bills every night."

"The money doesn't matter."

"What do you mean, *the money doesn't matter*?"

Before this morning, Kate never would have made such a bold claim. She lived in a two-and-a-half-room apartment above the town's only bookshop. A broken lock barely kept her door closed and she existed on a steady diet of diner food and gas station salad bowls. If anyone knew the importance of money and the detriment of not having it, it was Kate. But when faced with Clark, she didn't see a rich man or a happy one. He was someone desperate to hide his own crippling solitary confinement. He believed himself above Christmas because he believed himself above people in general, a fact Kate was out to prove completely false.

"It doesn't. I mean, I thought it did, but there's something there. Or, something isn't there. And if we can give it to him…"

Michael nodded and helped himself to the opposite end of the piano bench as Kate continued to noodle some random melodies. She operated on muscle memory, barely pressing the keys for noise.

"He may just want to give us the festival," he said.

"And he'll be a better man for it."

Michael huffed a noise under his breath. Clearly, transforming Clark into a better man ranked low on his list of priorities. For a while, nothing passed between them but the music pouring from her fingers. Kate recalled Clark's enraged voice when he heard the music upon first entering the house. Once he heard the live thing, it would only be a matter of time before he sprinted down here to stop her. Then, she'd have him right where she wanted him. Michael gave her an unreadable look, creeping into the corners of her vision like rolling fog.

"If I didn't know better, I'd say you like him."

Kate choked on her own laughter. Clark Woodward was arrogant. Prideful. A complete miser with no regard for the happiness or safety of others. He was a tyrannical boss and a rude host. And he'd never read Dickens. Who graduated with an MBA without reading Charles Dickens at least once? She couldn't ever see herself liking someone who hadn't read the greatest in the English canon, even if he did light a fire of excitement in her every time they began one of their verbal sparring matches.

"I don't like him."

"Hmm."

"I don't dislike him either!" She covered for herself, resisting the urge to hold up her hands in a pose of joking surrender. "I feel—"

Michael cut her off.

"You feel for him."

"I feel *bad* for him," she corrected, even though it wasn't remotely true. Or, rather, it was true, but it wasn't the entire truth. She did feel bad for him. It just wasn't the end of her feelings. Horror of horrors, she actually related to him. "Haven't you ever felt lonely?"

"Well, besides sharing a house with two brothers, I've had to deal with you basically my entire life. You never stop talking. No, I've never felt lonely."

"I have," Kate said, her head dipping down towards the piano keys.

"I know." Hard edges softened around Michael and he nodded in recognition. They would never speak of the thing that made her lonely, and he knew it. "I know. Just seems like a flimsy reason for you to want to help a guy."

"I can help him and the town at the same time. Those aren't mutually exclusive."

"I just want you to keep your eye on the ball," Michael said.

Kate didn't want to think about the sad things anymore. She wanted to sing. She wanted to play the piano until the lonely man upstairs was forced to confront them down here. She couldn't save the person she was when she was at her loneliest, but she could at least save him.

And her entire town and way of life, while she was at it.

With a blistering, face-cutting smile, Kate effectively ended their conversation.

"What do you think? 'Good King Wenceslas' or 'Here We Come A-Caroling?'"

After storming out of the room, Clark made a deal with himself: if he could survive the next two days without seeing Kate Buckner again, he would buy himself something nice. Something practical, of course. A watch, maybe. Or a new set of locks for his apartment in Dallas. A pair of shoes he didn't have to repair every other week because they insisted on falling apart at the seams when he walked too long or the temperature rose over seventy degrees. He rarely promised himself these sorts of rewards. His idea of a reward was sleeping in an extra fifteen minutes past his 6 a.m. alarm on Saturdays. But between the difficulty—maybe the impossibility—of avoiding Kate in his own house and the post-Christmas deals soon to flood the malls and shops back home, he decided it was worth it.

Here we come a-caroling along the fields so green!
Here we come wandering so fair to be seen!

He was sure he could do it until she started singing. There was music in his house. Not just any kind of music. Christmas music. When choosing a place to work from today, he'd made sure to pick the farthest room in the house from the living room. The second office used to host his uncle's secretary, if the discarded paperwork and bubble gum wrappers were any indication, and he assumed it would be a fine hideout for a few days. Its couch and proximity to a bathroom were convenient; he'd just have to make sure he snuck to the kitchen for snacks when he was sure Kate wasn't anywhere along his route.

A flawless plan...until she decided to go and fill the house with music. At first, Clark did his best to ignore it. He shut the heavy office door carefully, trying not to disturb the cheesy toy basketball hoop hung over the top—apparently, his uncle had hired an eight-year-old boy as a secretary—and returned to the whirring laptop. Maybe no one in this town was working, but he had a work ethic, and it didn't disappear because the weather got a little cold.

The closed door did basically nothing to prevent the music. If anything, it somehow managed to get louder. He shook his head and resolved to ignore it. He could manage distractions. He was disciplined enough to work over some annoying piano tunes.

Love and joy come to you! And to you glad Christmas too!

Clark tapped his foot. Maybe that sound would drown out their warbling.

And God bless you and se-end you a Happy New Year!

It didn't. He just managed to tap in time with them, giving them a beat. He covered his ears. Maybe *that* would drown them out.

And God se-end you a Happy Ne-ew Year!

It didn't. There was no drowning them out. Them, of course, because, as it turned out, he and Kate hadn't been as alone in the house as he assumed they were. Michael's slight drawl joined Kate's…competent singing. In a more generous mood, Clark might have described her singing as beautiful. Stirring, even. Not because it was technically perfect—it wasn't—but because there was a freedom to it. She didn't care about sounding good; she sang because it brought her joy.

Or something. Clark didn't want to read too deeply into it.

"That's enough."

Decorations and other passive, ignorable expressions of her Christmas obsession, he could handle. But indoor caroling? He couldn't allow it.

Leaving his work behind, he stormed downstairs. He flew past the miniature Dickens village set up on a long end table in the hallway, the popcorn garlands strung between overhead light fixtures, and down the garland-strewn grand staircase. Thank goodness his allergies didn't include pine or he'd be a dead man walking.

By the time he arrived in the living room, embarrassingly out of breath, they'd moved onto the slower, more somber "Silent Night," which Kate elected to sing in German.

Great. She knew German. The enemy living in his house was clever, talented, beautiful, *and* bilingual.

Not that Clark cared about any of that, of course. She was, above all, a nuisance. An obstacle to be conquered on his way to full control over his family's affairs. He had to think of her that way. He never thought about anyone else he did business with in warm or familiar terms. Why should he start now?

"What is this?"

"We're singing."

Apparently, the concept of a rhetorical question was lost on Michael, who answered with a big grin as Kate's song continued. Her head hung low over the keys and her golden-brown hair curtained her face, but the melody her lips offered wrapped around Clark with the insistence of prayer. He tried his best to ignore the clenching of his heart. The scene in the living room was something out of *The Saturday Evening Post*. Norman Rockwell couldn't have painted it better himself. A man and a woman sat, cozily enough, on a piano bench in the middle of a Christmas-covered living room. The fireplace crackled and the music hummed.

The picture-perfect image was enough to make Clark sick. It was enough to make Clark want to sing along. It was enough to make him wonder if Michael and Kate were together.

Again, not because he cared. Just because he needed more ammo against her. And he was curious.

"Singing's not allowed," he snapped, harsher than he intended.

Michael scoffed, undeterred.

"What is this, *The Sound of Music*?"

"I'm being pretty generous, letting you stay here. But this isn't an open invitation. You can't just have free rein in my house. And you know what?"

Clark's admittedly self-righteous lecture ended with the abrupt ringing of the doorbell. Truth be told, he was so oblivious to the workings of the house, he hadn't realized what their doorbell even sounded like, so the noise sent him jumping in shock.

"Oh, good!" Kate looked up from the piano keys for the first time since he arrived, her brown eyes alchemizing to a glistening gold. Michael popped up from the piano bench and ran towards the front door. For all of the excitement, a pit of understanding bottomed out in Clark's stomach. If he wasn't careful, his house would soon be overrun with townies. "Emily's here!"

"Emily who?"

"Emily Richards."

"I don't know who that is."

He didn't need an introduction. Emily Richards tottered through the living room door, juggling storage containers of brightly wrapped presents in her cocktail-straw-thin arms. The introduction wasn't necessary because Clark had actually met Emily the night before. She worked behind the check-in desk of the Miller's Point Bed and Breakfast. She was the one who had suggested sleeping in his car because "no one in this town is going to have room for you after what you did."

He hadn't taken her advice, choosing instead to return home for the first time in a long time, but that didn't stop her words and the hatred in her eyes from haunting him the entire way.

Emily Richards was a twig of a woman with high blonde hair. She couldn't have been any more different from Kate if she tried. Where Kate was all curves and warmth, Emily was narrow and icy. Without knowing either of them particularly well, Clark could only assume their differences made their friendship work.

"Sorry I'm late. I walked all the way up the hill and it was *murder* on my calves. Where should I put these?"

"What are those?"

"Donation bins." Kate's deft hands continued their musical exploration of the keyboard, even as she afforded him the bare minimum of her attention in favor of Emily. "Go ahead and put them on the floor for now. We'll take them out with us later."

"Later? Where are you going?"

The suspense extended as Emily flounced into his kitchen without saying so much as a "hello" to him.

"Who wants eggnog?" she shouted.

"Three glasses in here please!"

Nope. Clark's foot needed to come down. He couldn't allow them to walk all over him and around him like this. He'd given her the run of the house, sure. But he did not agree to have his entire life overrun, not by Kate and certainly not by her friends. Every minute, she threw more and more illegal fireworks at him; soon, his annoyance would explode. His right hand twitched; he struggled to control his own breathing.

No one got under his skin like this. Not business partners, not rivals. And never a woman.

"No, no! No eggnog for me. Two glasses."

"But—"

"I didn't come down here for eggnog. I came down here to tell you to stop playing."

"It's not Christmas without music. C'mon," she said, her voice lighter than a chorus of bells. "Sing a song with us. It'll be fun."

"I don't sing," he growled.

"Everyone sings at Christmas," Kate said. Emily returned with the eggnog and requisitioned the overstuffed couch, plopping down on it and burying herself in the cushions. "Even Frank Sinatra sang Christmas songs and he could hardly carry a tune."

"Frank Sinatra was a *great* singer and this isn't a party!"

"Why not?" Her golden eyes twinkled with the edges of a private joke. "You look like you could use a little party." She'd wedged herself under his skin and she knew it.

You look like you could use a little party. The challenge repeated in his head, a maddening, singsong refrain he wished he could pluck out and erase from his memory. An unfamiliar feeling welled inside of him; every time he tried to place it, the name eluded him. It wasn't rage or dignified coldness; he could easily identify those, as they were his most common emotional responses to nearly any annoyance, even if he didn't let them register on his face. He felt altogether different than he could ever remember feeling before.

Fondness? Was it fondness?

Before he could answer, he turned tail. A hasty retreat would be best. Alone in his office, there was no way he could feel anything for Kate.

"I have to work. Keep the noise down and the disasters to a minimum, please," he commanded.

But he'd only made it three steps towards the exit when Michael sidled up beside him and dropped his voice to a conspiratorial whisper. Clark didn't often have occasion to feel like "one of the boys," but when Michael elbow nudged him, he could almost imagine it.

"Hey, Clark."

"Yes?"

"Can I give you some advice?"

Clark didn't want his advice. He knew the other man's advice would inevitably lead him to staying here, in this room, in close proximity to the undecorated Christmas tree and the beautiful, determined, open-hearted Kate Buckner.

"…Yes."

"Just go along for the ride. Your life will be much, *much* easier. I promise."

He huffed out a breath and scanned the room again. The living room of Woodward House always sunk under the weight of its own grandeur. Its stark beauty reflected its self-importance in its thick brocade furnishings and expensive finishes. The entire house suffered this design style; the office Clark holed himself up in, untouched by Kate's magical Christmas hands, was a sea of dark shadows and leather chairs. He glanced around this room. The new décor was— dare he say it?—tasteful. Small touches of holiday décor accented the mantelpieces and end tables, while a simple wreath hung above the fireplace. Even the Christmas tree was mercifully undecorated, strung with only simple garlands of white fairy lights. On the one hand, he resented the intrusion of brightness and levity to his dark world. On the other, could he really go back to his small room and listen to their laughter and song, knowing all the while he could be a part of it if he only said yes? Was he really content to sit in the darkness when light was just a step away? He knew he couldn't return to the shadows.

He just didn't want anyone else to know that.

Besides, the threat of memories in this place was too strong. Every corner of this house reminded him of the time *before*, of when he had a family here, when this season actually meant something to him. If he stayed here with Kate and her friends, then at least he'd have a distraction.

Steady as a tree, he returned to the fold of the living room party. He never once let his expression slip, but Kate seemed to see straight through him, as she had from the moment they met. She didn't look at him with judgment, though. There was something else in her soft tone. Understanding? Acceptance?

Clark couldn't tell, and maybe he didn't want to. All he wanted was one uncomplicated day in the sun.

"Any requests?" she asked.

"I'm not singing. But I will stay." He tacked on another claim, just in case she thought she'd won something in this exchange. "Just to make sure you don't burn the house down."

A single nod and quiet smile were his only reward from Kate.

Emily picked up the slack. Popping up from the couch, she declared, "Great idea. I'll get you some eggnog after all."

Chapter Six

Halfway through "Good King Wenceslas," the clock above the fireplace struck noon, sending a chorus of chiming bells announcing the time into the room and disturbing the natural melody of their carol. If all had actually gone to plan and Michael hadn't screwed the entire thing up, they would have just been welcoming Clark to the house right about now.

Kate structured her original plan, with its intricate, timed details, to act in the same manner as a whirlwind. They were meant to sweep Clark from one themed activity to another, whipping him into a happy Yuletide frenzy. She'd added Christmas caroling as a last-minute effort to kill time before Emily arrived, and though it wasn't a part of the original plan, Kate thought it fit right in. Clark stood at the end of the piano, doing his best to look every bit as stoic as a Mr. Darcy reenactor, but every once in a while, Kate would look up at him from under her eyelashes and catch him mouthing a phrase of a song before catching himself and pretending it never happened.

He thought no one saw his slip-ups. He was wrong. Kate caught them, and they fanned the flames of hope in her heart, for her plan and for him. She tried her best to hide her triumphant smile behind a curtain of hair. Spooking him could lead to disaster; she had to play her cards right if she wanted him to keep opening up.

In the middle of the song, Emily shot to her feet, checking her phone's clock against the one on the wall.

"That's the time? Kate, we've got to go if we want to make it."

"Make it where? Where are you going?"

If Kate didn't know better—and to be totally honest, she *didn't* know better—she would have sworn she heard a whimper of disappointment in Clark's voice, but she dismissed the thought as soon as it came through her head. Sure, maybe some of his edges had softened. Flickers of humanity peeked out from behind his stony exterior. That didn't mean he was suddenly an avid caroler, nor did he enjoy her company and want her to stay.

A stupid and exceptionally loud part of Kate's brain desperately wanted to hear what Clark's singing voice sounded like. Would it be thick and deep? Tenor and sweet? Would he be able to sing on key at all? She realized what a small thing it was, to want to know how someone sang, but she couldn't help wanting it all the same. In her experience, though, the smallest things were always the hardest to get in this life.

"Christmas isn't just a day for eating and eggnog," she said, leaving the piano and her dreams of hearing Clark sing behind.

"Though eggnog is a big part of it," Michael joked.

"It's also," Kate said through a laugh, "a day to do good."

"Well," Clark corrected.

"Not well. *Good*. Miller's Point is a great town, but there are still plenty of families that need our help. Every year on Christmas Eve, we do a big donation of Christmas presents and provisions for them, but no festival means no place to give out the donations, so a couple of us volunteered to pick up the slack."

One of the first thoughts Kate had after his announcement was for those families. Money was tight for her, but for some, it was even worse. Miller's Point wasn't a big town by any stretch of the imagination, and they didn't have a poverty epidemic like Clark might have seen in Dallas, but the few who needed help still mattered. If she couldn't at least help them, what good was she to anyone else? Kate reached for her coat as Michael and Emily started collecting the heavy boxes of presents waiting on the floor.

"We'll be gone for about an hour," she informed him as she wrapped herself in her favorite soft red scarf. Miss Carolyn knit it for her last year, and though it was full of holes and missed stitches, Kate couldn't bear to leave home without it. "Are you going to change the locks while we're out?"

"I could come with you."

Kate blinked. The offer… It *sounded* generous and kind. Which couldn't be true because she wasn't sure Clark Woodward had a generous or kind bone in his body. Kate's pulse quickened.

"What?"

"It's…" He cleared his throat. "Your things are heavy. I could drive you, I mean. That way you don't have to carry them back down the hill."

"Really?"

"It would be easier than taking this down by ourselves," Michael offered, though his skepticism was plainly written on every corner of his face.

"It will be good," Clark said. "You know, for the people in town to get to know me."

…*Before you take their jobs away.* Kate struggled with this Clark Woodward character. Every time she thought she got him, every time she saw some light poking out through the cracks in his walls, she remembered why she was here in the first place. He was close to destroying the town, trying to take away everything they held dear.

She wanted to see the best in him, and more than anything she wanted to find a way to make him happy in the same way his family had made this town happy for so many years. And yet…he seemed to go out of his way to make himself out to be the biggest jerk around. Until now. Until this moment.

"All right." Kate handed him one of the crates, groaning under its weight. What had they bought these kids, lead bricks? "Take this. And pull the car around. We'll be out in a minute."

They departed. Emily and Kate remained in the living room. When the door closed behind the two men, signaling that they were really alone, Emily's mouth popped into a perfect O and her eyes widened with fake horror.

"Wow. He's…"

Kate held up a silencing hand. She didn't need to like Clark to make her plan work, but she *wanted* to like Clark. No one deserved to be miserable at Christmas, not even the very cruel, but it would make things so much easier if she felt he had even a chance of being a good man.

"I've never heard you say a bad thing about another person. Don't start now."

"That's not true. You've heard me say many bad things about many people. Most people, actually."

"Still."

"I wasn't going to say anything *bad* about him. Just…"

"Just what?"

Emily's hesitation spoke louder than any condemnation ever could. She was one of the most passive-aggressive, backhanded-compliment people Kate ever knew. You'd be on the receiving end of the world's most beautiful smile while being told you were a moron, but she'd say it so you thought she was lavishing praise on you. In the end, she picked up a storage tub, shook her head once, and said in the most piteous voice Kate ever heard:

"Bless his heart."

Even if Clark hadn't told her he'd rented this car, Kate could have guessed it. The sleek silver car hid a leather interior with a control panel so futuristic it might as well have been ripped out of a *Star Trek* ship. She could imagine him driving around Dallas in a usually broken-down clunker before she could imagine him forking over the thousands of dollars this car probably cost.

In the front seat, Michael guided Clark down the hill and the twisting, turning roads leading them to the back roads of Miller's Point. Out here, things were even quieter than in town, if such a thing were possible. Kate's request to turn the radio to 109.7, the local station that played *all the holiday hits from yesterday and today*, was firmly denied, and they rode into town in total silence, save for Michael's occasional navigation tips.

"Yeah, and just pull in here."

They turned up the familiar drive to the Lewisham house, where little Bradley and his family would be waiting for them. Sure enough, when they passed the tree line towards their humble house, Bradley sat on the front steps, tapping his feet and twiddling the famous

Tiny Tim cane. Apparently, last night no one had the heart to tell him he couldn't bring the costumes home. Kate's gaze flickered to Clark. Was he heartless enough to take a fake cane worth less than three dollars from a little boy?

Probably not... Right?

Before the car even lurched to a stop, Bradley launched himself at it, shouting Kate's name as loud as he could. It was a good thing no one else lived out here, or he'd be disturbing the entire neighborhood.

"Miss Kate! Miss Kate!"

No matter how many times she heard it, she always got a thrill of the maternal every time one of the children in the festival called out to her. Leaving the donation tub behind her, she leapt out of the car and scooped him into her arms, hugging him tight.

"How's it going, Bradley?"

Bradley, as it turned out, wasn't interested in telling her about his day. Missing front tooth and all, he spluttered, "Are we going back? Is the festival back on again? Do I need to go get my hat?"

The belief in his eyes that everything was set right again stabbed a knife straight between her eyes. This boy with the saucer-big brown eyes believed she had the power to wave a magic wand and make everything well again.

She hoped she could prove him right.

"No, buddy. We're still working all of that out, but—"

"Will you tell me why?"

Still holding him in her arms—he was too big for it, but she indulged him anyway—Kate turned to watch the movement in the car.

"Sure. I'll tell you as soon as I can."

"Good. Because I have been working on my accent and," he dropped into a thick and terrible Cockney accent, "I fink it's going swell, I do!"

He continued speaking in his accent, but her mind wandered. By the end of the afternoon, if they kept to their plans, they'd visit four houses with presents while a second group visited later in the evening with hot meals and frozen, reheatable food for the next day. If the festival had been going on, the food would have been served at the event and the presents doled out on Christmas morning, but given the unexpected changes, that morning they'd devised a new plan. In some ways, this might be better. More personal. On the other hand, Kate knew how deeply these families hated anything remotely resembling charity. In the friendly environment of the festival, where huge buffets of turkey and sweet potato pie ran through town hall like a deliciously fattening river, no one felt they were accepting charity because everyone shared equally. Bringing a bunch of food directly to a family with maybe six or seven days off a year so that they could spend their precious time together instead of cooking was targeted, singling out the people who needed the most help.

By the time she turned to the car, it was empty.

Well, empty except for one.

Clark, for his part, hadn't moved away from the car at all. He leaned against the hood, reading something on his phone and determinedly not looking anywhere but the dimmed screen. There was a strange duality to Clark. On the one hand, he clearly lived a frugal, tight-fisted existence. On the other hand, he had every luxury and advantage at his fingertips. He should have been a snob. Being a snob definitely would have explained his refusal to even interact with the Lewisham family or their aging but proudly kept home. There were only two motives she could see for keeping himself away from the people he'd driven here to help.

A) He was an unsalvageable, irreversible, cruel man beyond salvation, who hated the poor, resented the working, and slept happily on stacks of money. He had to rest up, naturally, because he spent his days diving into money bins full of gold coins. Or:

B)…Something else. She wasn't entirely sure what that something else was, but there *had* to be a second option. She refused to see the worst of him and only the worst. Maybe he was allergic to the wildflowers in the front lawn? Maybe he didn't want to rub his wealth in their face?

She looked at his face. Tight. Strained. Maybe he was nervous?

"Hey, Bradley?"

"Yep!"

She released him; he plopped to the ground with the lightest thud she ever heard. Like a dedicated method actor, he leaned against his Tiny Tim cane, putting all his weight on it. Kate bent down to his eye level; she needed to impress upon him the importance of this mission. Just one little interaction could be the key to understanding the bank vault of a man who'd driven her here.

"If you do something for me, I promise I'll tell you everything. Deal?"

"Deal." Bradley brandished his cane like a sword. "Now, who do I have to fight?"

"You don't have to fight anyone. You see that guy over there?"

"Yeah."

"His name is Clark, and—"

"I know who he is!"

"Okay. Okay! What do you think about him?"

"He looks kind of lonely." Bradley shrugged. He matched his voice to the whisper of Kate's, keeping his tone low and confidential. "He's not your boyfriend, is he? Because everyone hates him."

Hate. What a bold, uncompromising word for a nine-year-old. A shiver gripped Kate's spine. The hairs on her neck raised.

"We don't hate him. We have to *help* him. Can you go over there and just…" She searched for the words to describe what she wanted. In the end, she landed on the one thing *she* wanted to do. "Just be nice to him?"

Bradley's face scrunched as he leaned on his cane, giving him the appearance of a curmudgeonly old man. A mini Scrooge. Of all the times not to have a camera handy.

"What, just like talk to him and stuff?"

"You said he looks lonely. Go be a friend."

"But everyone hates him! Everyone'll hate me next."

Hate, hate, hate. That wasn't Christmas talk at all. That wasn't Miller's Point talk. Kate couldn't let the poison of fear infect her town any more than it already had.

There was only one thing to do now: talk to the small child as though they were secret agents.

"No one's going to be mad..." She looked left, then right, as if checking for spies. "You're helping with the plan."

"What plan?"

"The *secret* plan to get the festival back. I can't tell you the specifics until you finish this mission. I have to know you can be trusted."

"Deal." Bradley started for the car, but stopped so hard he created a dust cloud. "And I want a candy bar."

"You can have a stick of gum."

He beamed.

"Deal."

⁕

Clark didn't often make bad decisions. At least, he told himself he never made bad decisions. Before coming to Miller's Point, the last bad thing he did was choose the cranberry orange protein bars instead of the blueberry protein bars during his last grocery shop.

But upon arriving at Miller's Point, he seemed incapable of making good decisions. Leaving his car on the street to get towed? Bad call. Letting Kate talk down to him on his first night? *Really* bad call. Giving Kate free rein over his family's house? Terrible call. Coming along on this charity mission? The worst call.

Like most things—including the cranberry orange bars, which had fifteen fewer calories than the blueberry—it started with good intentions. Good, stupid intentions. That was the reason Clark tried his best *never* to do anything with good intentions. He preferred neutral intentions. Good intentions always backfired. Neutral intentions weren't capable of backfiring, because no one had any skin in the game.

This decision was innocent and knee-jerk. He saw her struggling under the weight of packages, fighting to hold them upright, and eventually falling right down the steep hill from the Woodward House into town. He imagined being called to the hospital and having to identify her scraped-up face—a ridiculous thought, of course, since he would have been the last person she ever listed as an emergency contact. However absurd, the horrible images wouldn't leave his head, so he volunteered to drive her and her friends.

Now, he was here, in front of a tiny shack of a home. The second he pulled the key out of the ignition and got a good view of the place, not to mention the little boy with the Tiny Tim cane sprinting into Kate's arms, a swirling hurricane drew all of the energy from Clark's body and concentrated it in the pit of his stomach. His palms grew clammy, and as soon as he was finished carrying the heavy tub of general sundry and supplies up to the porch, he slipped on a reliably dark pair of sunglasses and focused his attention on his phone.

He knew how it looked. They would think him standoffish and rude, superior and arrogant. He'd rather they think that than know the truth.

The truth was…he'd taken something important away from these people. The festival was stupid as far as he was concerned, but it clearly meant more to them than he realized…

He was used to being hated. Hatred was the cost of doing business. But hatred was always a distant thing brought on by business decisions. It wasn't up close. Personal.

When he came to town, he'd assumed he could hide from people. Dissolving the company would be easy enough; he was the boss. No one could openly hate the boss. But here at someone else's house, the house of a family who clearly loved the festival…

He couldn't face them. Hence the sunglasses. And the phone. And general *please don't come near me* vibe.

So, it surprised him when a small child ran up and stood beside him.

"Hey."

Clark did not respond.

"Hey, guy."

The child tugged on Clark's suit jacket. Still, he did not respond.

"Hey!"

When children shout, there's no choice but to respond. Raising one eyebrow over the top ridge of his pitch-black sunglasses, Clark glanced down.

"Yes?"

"My name's Bradley. And you're Clark Woodward, right?"

"Mm-hm."

He pocketed his cellphone. There was no reason to invest his time in this kid at all, but it would be worse to ignore him and have him run up to the house screaming about the mean man outside. Clark believed in his ability to be minimally polite.

"I knew that was your name. I'm really good at remembering stuff. That's why I got the part of Tiny Tim. I can remember all the lines. And I have a *ton* of lines. I'm good at remembering stuff and I'm really short. And poor. I guess it's at least a little bit because we're poor. I really get the Tiny Tim *thing*, you know?"

"Mm-hm." Clark bit his bottom lip to keep from laughing. Bradley was a character. It didn't surprise him he got cast as the lead in this town-wide play. His little face expressed a range of emotions in a second. The little boy huffed and leaned on some kind of roughly carved wooden walking stick. Not being familiar with the Dickens canon, Clark was vaguely aware the Tiny Tim character was disabled... Was this boy *also* injured, or did he just not want to let the role go?

"You're not making this very easy."

"Making what easy?"

With his free, non-walking-stick hand, Bradley smacked his face and sighed. Clark called him a character, but "ham" would have been more accurate.

"Miss Kate said I could have a candy bar if I came over and made you happy but you're not making it easy. Well, she actually said I could have a stick of gum. I don't think Miss Kate can afford candy bars either."

Ignoring Kate's desire to make him happy for the moment, he caught instead on the insinuation of her poverty. She was clean and well-dressed. Her boots were scuffed and strained from wear, but that could just as easily be explained as she loved them too much to get rid of them, rather than them being the only shoes she owned or could afford to own.

"Why's that?"

"She lost her job when you cancelled the festival. It was kind of her life. She was the youngest person to work there, you know."

This is exactly why Clark avoided children. They didn't know anything about tact or keeping secrets or not punching their conversation partners in the stomach with their words. The only thing Clark knew concretely about Kate's relationship with the festival was that she loved it. Having deliberately kept his attention in the business to non-Christmas matters when his uncle was alive, he hadn't taken a look at the employee roster yet or familiarized himself with their staff, so he didn't know she worked there. Or that it was her life.

He didn't know, and he didn't want to know. *Change the subject, Clark. Change the subject.*

"Stay here for one second."

"Where're you going?"

Back in his car, Clark dove for the glove compartment. He usually took pride in its perfect organization—he liked his registration and safety manual where he could easily get them—but today he needed the one bit of clutter shoved in it. A white plastic bag with a blue outline of a tooth stamped on it. Out of that baggie came a silver-wrapped chocolate bar. Clark returned and handed it over to the wide-eyed boy.

"I got this at the dentist office the other day."

"You dentist gives you *candy*?"

"All dentist offices are rackets. They give you candy so you have to go right back and get more fillings. Make sure you brush your teeth."

Bradley ripped away the wrapping like a Roald Dahl character. He tore into the chocolate. Clark couldn't help but wonder when the child last had a dentist appointment. If they couldn't buy their own Christmas presents in a Christmas-obsessed town, who's to say they had enough money for dental work?

"Yes, sir. I will, sir." Bradley smacked his lips as he chewed, a pet peeve of Clark's he decided to ignore for the moment. After a contemplative silence, Bradley swallowed and spoke again. "You know...you're kinda like him."

"Like who?"

"Scrooge."

Clark didn't even have time to absorb the blow of those words. Kate interrupted their chat with Michael and Emily in tow.

"I think we're all done here."

Tucking his cane under his chocolate-holding arm, he held up his free hand.

"Gum, please."

"You think you earned it?" Kate chuckled. The sound was better than music. "He's not even smiling."

"C'mon, Mr. Clark. Give her a smile."

No. A line in the sand needed to be drawn. He'd been...polite to the boy and he was going to be stuck with Kate for the next thirty-six hours or so. None of them were going to walk away from this conversation thinking he could be manipulated. Not by gap-toothed children with chocolate-covered hands or beautiful women with laughter like wind chimes on a sunny beach.

"I'm not a trained animal. I don't smile on command."

The little boy dug his heels in to argue, but a call from his father on the porch rescued Clark from any kind of debate.

"Bradley! Come in here and help your sisters set the table."

The boy groaned. Kate knelt down and handed him the stick of gum. In another scenario, Clark would have protested. He didn't earn the gum, and what kind of lesson was she teaching him if she gave him things he didn't earn? Maybe *that* was the problem with this town. Everyone here was too soft, too afraid of hurting feelings to say no.

"Here's your gum. Merry Christmas, B."

But…even he had to admit how sweet Kate looked as she ruffled Bradley's hair and sent him on his way. As he walked towards his tiny house, he gave one last goodbye.

"God bless us, everyone."

It didn't take a master of subtext to read into his declaration. *God bless everyone. Even you, Mr. Clark.* Once he disappeared behind the faded red door, Kate turned on him.

"You couldn't have even smiled for him?"

He didn't realize how long he'd been staring into the depths of her eyes, catching the flickers of mixing colors and light in her pointed gaze. When had she gotten so close? And why did he want to be closer? His gaze flickered down to her lips. Just a breath closer, just a heartbeat nearer to her and they'd be less than a kiss apart. And it shocked him how dearly he suddenly wanted that in this moment.

He coughed. Stepped away. And shook his head.

"No. No, I couldn't."

"What a shame." She smiled, a tease hiding in the corner of her mouth. "I bet you have a nice smile."

He coughed again and put as much distance between them as he could, flexing and clenching his hand. The movement of muscles in his fingers did nothing to quell his desire to take her hand and hold it in his. As they got in the car, Clark recalled thinking coming to this house and meeting these people was the worst thing he'd done in recent memory. He knew now that wasn't true.

The worst thing he had done since arriving in Miller's Point was almost kissing Kate.

Or not kissing her.

He couldn't decide which was worse.

Chapter Seven

The afternoon rolled past Clark in a flurry of cold, slushy rain and tittering laughter and conversation. He drove them to their next few stops, but no longer got out of the car. He considered it a strategic move. They would be safe from any near-miss kisses if he did the noble thing of helping to bring the boxes to the door and immediately returning to the safety of his car. Insulated by the steel and leather interior, he couldn't hear her laugh or smell the nutmeg in her hair. Every once in a while, his attention snagged on bits of conversation muttered outside of his window. Mostly insults about him. *Why are you hanging out with that scumbag? Makes sense he wouldn't want to come in and touch us poors. If I didn't respect his uncle so much, I'd take him out back and give him what for.*

Every year, *Texas Magazine* ranked the towns and cities of the state by the kindness and friendliness of their citizens. Miller's Point regularly came in at

#1. The nicest people in the entire state hated him. Normally, he didn't mind hatred. He tried not to mind it now, but he couldn't help but think, *I don't want Kate to hate me.*

When he didn't catch them saying cruel and utterly justified things about his character, Clark captured little glimpses into the life of the woman who'd singlehandedly invaded his life. *Thank you so much for bringing my boy to the doctor last week. I couldn't have gotten the time off.* Or, *you'll never believe what happened last week! I took your advice and asked Laura out at her favorite place at the festival and she said yes! We're going out next week for New Year's.* Kate invested herself in these people, and not just for cheap displays of her own dedication to charity. Clark couldn't name a single neighbor in his apartment building, while Kate consistently remembered birthdays, anniversaries, breakups, and the name of every single person she came across. Small-town living came with perks and privileges not enjoyed by city folk like him, but he didn't suspect everyone in Miller's Point—or any small town for that matter—acted exactly like her. She was a creature entirely unto herself. He'd yet to meet anyone on earth, much less in Miller's Point, who rivaled Kate in any way.

Whether that was a point in her favor or a demerit, he couldn't be entirely sure.

The car's bells chimed as the doors opened and the ragtag team of daylight Santas, now relieved of their boxes and presents, slipped inside.

"That was the last one," Kate said.

Clark turned the key in the ignition and headed for town. Driving around today gave him a much better sense of the place, all of its hidden side streets and tangled roundabouts. Cell service cut out all over town, making his cell phone directions absolutely useless. Upon first arriving in Miller's Point, the maps would disappear and reappear at will, sending him on crazy routes until he finally gave up. Finding the town square last night was nothing short of a miracle.

Michael, on the other hand, knew every inch of Miller's Point and didn't require battery life or WiFi.

Conversation flowed easily between the three friends, leaving Clark to feel a bit like an out-of-the-loop Uber driver, an experience he only knew from the one time his bike got a flat tire in downtown Dallas and the public transportation workers spent the day on strike, forcing him to use the car-sharing service. In a city with plenty of bike racks and trams, Clark saw no reason to pay seven bucks for someone else to ferry him around.

"Wanna stop somewhere and get lunch?" Michael asked. "I'm starving."

"You're always starving."

"No one is starving. We all ate this morning."

"We could go to the diner."

"It's closed."

"You were literally there this morning."

"Mel opened it special for Kate and Clark sneaked in. Mel felt too bad to tell him to get lost."

The tips of Clark's ears reddened. He hadn't even noticed a *closed* sign. Was he really so entitled that he just waltzed in and assumed he'd be served?

"No." Kate inserted herself into her friends' conversation. Calm before the storm. "We can go back to Woodward."

Oh, no. That sounded like trouble. To Clark's knowledge, the kitchen hadn't been stocked since the last time his uncle visited the place. What was she planning to feed him? Canned chicken and bagged rice?

"What's at Woodward?" he asked, failing to hide his suspicion.

"You'll see," Kate replied.

"I'd really like to know…"

"You'll see."

He swallowed hard as the town passed by around him. Possibilities ricocheted against the walls of his skull. Was she going to make him go into the woods and kill a wild turkey or put him on a cabbage soup diet? Television ads around this time of year and NPR podcast sponsors assured him everyone ate instant stuffing and probably turkey for their holiday meal, but having eaten grilled cheese or zucchini lasagna on this day the last three or four years, he couldn't be entirely certain.

"I don't like surprises."

"Really?" Emily snarked. "You seem like such a zany, seat-of-your-pants kind of guy."

The burn effectively silenced Clark. No one was

going to take his side in this. The urge to retort pried open his jaw, but when nothing came to mind, he closed it again. The board room at Woodward Headquarters had sharpened his wit, sure. Only no one there dared to take jabs at him. He mostly swung his verbal sword in their direction, not the other way around.

Knowing his own way back now, he turned into the town square. Without the festival, the streets opened themselves to cars again. In Dallas, the people would have thanked him for giving them the streets back, but not in Miller's Point. Driving through the square gave off an almost eerie, end-of-the-world vibe. Half of the decorations were gone—most likely taken down to be strung up in his house—and the sidewalks sat empty and unused. The tree, a monstrosity of fir and ornaments he couldn't even begin to calculate a cost for, lorded over the square, dark and unlit. Eerie, even for someone who hated this holiday and everything it stood for. The silence probably didn't help. Clark usually drove to NPR and various podcasts about business and finance, but after they'd asked for Christmas music he'd panicked and said he preferred to concentrate on the road.

When they started talking again, he'd have given anything for the sweet release of some kind of background noise. Every word they uttered dug into his skin, sharpened arrows built to pierce him.

"I can't believe everything's over." Michael clucked. "No more festival."

"Don't say that. Anything can happen."

Kate's reply embodied everything Clark knew about her so far. Foolishly optimistic. Beautifully wasteful. What did she think, he was going to cave and give in to their ridiculous whims? Waste money on something he saw no value in? Or did she think some other millionaire investor would sweep in and take the loss? Not likely. He'd already warned potential investors off the project when he decided to close the place down. Even keeping the place open for a few more nights, the rest of their season, would waste money in personnel and electric bills.

They finished the ride home without incident… until they pulled up to the house, and Clark's worst fears about Kate's "surprise" came to life through the clear wall of his windshield. During their brief time in the wilds of Miller's Point, the long driveway had turned into a parking lot. At least thirty trucks and SUVs made themselves very much at home on the pavement stretching almost a hundred yards from the street to the carriage-house-turned-garage tucked away behind the manor.

Clark pulled through the center clearing—thank God someone gave a thought to how they would all get in and out—and fought the quiver of anger in his voice. *Control yourself, man. You have always been able to control yourself before. Why can't you control yourself around Kate?*

"What's all this?"

"You'll see when we get inside."

He parked and they headed for the back door of

the house, with Michael and Emily at the lead and him and Kate trailing behind. If Kate disturbed or confused them with this turn of events, they didn't let on. Clark didn't think anything about Kate would faze them by now. From what he'd seen of their friendship, Kate charged forward and everyone else hopped on board without a second thought. He secretly admired that about her.

"Why are there are people here?"

"You'll see. Just follow me. Everyone's inside."

Something strange happened then. Something Clark hadn't expected and didn't know he wanted. She reached for his hand, took it in her own, and led him forward. The contact didn't spark or crackle with electric shocks; the books and poems lied about that. She held his hand like she wanted to remember what it felt like. Like she wanted him to know every line in her palm and how her pulse danced against his. Holding hands with Kate Buckner was like falling into his own bed after a long day of work. A complete relief.

He ripped himself away, violently breaking up the sensation. It made Kate flinch, but her smile didn't falter or slip. She shook it off. She shook off everything he threw at her. He added another word to his description of her. *Endlessly* foolishly optimistic.

"I don't want people here. I told you this isn't a party."

Up the servant's steps and into the back hallway, Kate led him through the family house. How was it possible she knew this place better than he did? Up until his ninth birthday, he spent every Christmas here with his family. He should lead, not her.

"Okay," she began, popping with excited energy. "Every year, on Christmas Eve, we have a huge festival feast for lunch before we open the doors for the guests. I mean, it's huge. Everyone in town comes and we have everything you can imagine—"

"Last year, Buzz Schrute carved a Nativity scene out of butter. With a chainsaw," Michael called over his shoulder. They turned the corner to the main living wing, which housed the library, the study, the formal parlor, the living room, kitchens and formal dining room. The public wing of the house.

"Eating is as much a part of the Christmas experience as anything else. Everyone really opens up around the table. When you share a meal with someone, you're really sharing a part of your soul."

"Where are you going with this?"

They approached the formal dining room. *Oh, no.* The house no longer reeked of gingerbread or fir. Other smells swirled in dizzying circles around Clark's head. Garlic. Onions. Sage. Parsley. Paprika. Sweet potato. Brussels sprouts... Turkey.

"I wanted to show you what it's like. Give you a taste of the real Miller's Point Christmas experience. So, drumroll, please..." Kate shoved the French doors apart, revealing Clark's worst nightmare. He thought a redecorated house couldn't get any worse, but once again, Kate blew him and his expectations away.

"Surprise!"

The shout came not from Kate or her two compatriots, but from a room filled to the brim with Miller's Point Christmas nerds. In his rushed morning, Clark never inspected the formal dining room. He knew from his childhood that it accommodated almost forty-five people, though he'd never seen so many in there. Old, young, fat, thin, tall, short, black, white, in Christmas sweaters, in dresses. Everyone crammed around the table to surprise him and welcome him to his own personal brand of torture. Decorations covered the carved wood paneling of the walls and a miniature Christmas tree—apparently the towering monstrosity in the living room wasn't enough to sate Kate's lust for the noble fir—took post in the corner.

But ornate decorations were nothing compared to the table. Pages from Dr. Seuss stories were less cluttered and colorful. Anything ever featured on a Martha Stewart Thanksgiving special or on the cover of the November issue of *Southern Living* claimed space at this feast.

Stuffing. No fewer than six varieties of potato. Sweet potato casserole. Sweet potato biscuits. Green bean casserole. Cranberry sauce—homemade and canned. Cornbread. Corn pudding. Corn on the cob. Creamed corn. Mac 'n' cheese. Gravy. Brussels sprouts. Soup. Ham. Spinach dip. Broccoli salad. And on and on until the room nearly exploded with plate upon plate of delicious calories.

Three turkeys. Who needed one turkey, much less three?

It all looked so delicious. And so, so unnecessary. He clenched his jaw so tight he thought it might break his teeth.

"What is this?"

"It's a feast."

Kate joined the crowd, leaving him alone against a sea of strangers. He marveled. They all believed in this garbage. They all thought he would sit down at the table and suddenly be a changed man. Kate believed it. She was wrong. They were all wrong. He shoved his hands into his pockets so no one could spot their trembling.

"I can see that. Where did it all come from?"

"We ordered it. Well, some of it was already cooked and frozen for the feast, but we had to order some of it because—"

"Who paid for it?"

This time, Kate hesitated. The air in the room tightened, tense and uncomfortable. People shuffled, shifted their weight from one foot to the other, glanced uncertainly at Kate and coughed. With every tick of the grandfather clock placed against the far wall, as the inevitable explanation came closer and closer, Clark's pulse boomed in his ears. His right hand kept flexing and clenching against the lining of his suit pocket. One woman stepped back, apparently afraid he'd turn violent.

He wasn't a violent man, but he didn't rule out knocking over a gravy boat or two.

"It's part of the company expenses. We do this every year for the festival and—"

There it was. The explanation he knew was coming still managed to enrage him. His carefully constructed mask flew away, leaving nothing but the anger. He may have admired Kate, even liked her a bit, but she was still, at her core, stealing money from his company by disobeying his directive to cancel all festival-related orders. Stealing that which didn't belong to her all to prove some stupid point about a holiday he would *never* like.

"I'm dissolving the company because it's wasteful. This entire stupid holiday is a monument to *waste* and excess and it sickens me!"

A woman stepped forward, a coaxing but vain smile on her aging face.

"We worked really hard on this and—"

"Well that hard work was a waste of time because I'm not touching this. Go. Leave. Get out of here."

"Clark."

Kate threw him a lifeline. A chance to take it back and respond with a little bit of kindness. These people did nothing to him. They followed Kate and tried to help her. This was all her doing, really. He knew all of this intellectually, but his emotions either didn't get the memo or they got the memo and crumbled it into an unreadable ball before burning it.

"I didn't stutter. Get out of here."

When no one moved and all attention turned to

the dumbstruck and now decidedly unsmiling Kate Buckner, Clark repeated himself.

"Get. Out!"

With that, the great exodus began. Everyone practically ran for their dishes, picking up what they could and filing out through the connected kitchen door, carefully avoiding Clark, who stood in silent rage. He'd deal with Kate once everyone else left. Only a few stragglers remained when Emily squared off with him.

She was ready for a fight.

"Hey, man. You're being a real jerk, you know that?"

She passed passive-aggressive and dove straight for aggressive-aggressive. Clark didn't care. He could be aggressive too.

"Am I? I feel like someone entered my family's house without permission and spent our money on things I didn't approve after she knew how I felt about it. How am I the bad guy here?"

"Because Kate's trying to do something nice for you after you ruined Christmas. I don't know why she's going to the trouble. You're the *worst*."

"It would have been nice if she'd left me alone, which is what I wanted. And what I still want."

Only the four of them remained, though Clark didn't give Kate a second thought. Nothing mattered now but his own self-righteous frustrations. He opened his mouth to release even more steam, only to be cut off by Michael.

"You know what…" He ran a hand across his short-cut hair, fake sincerity dripping from every syllable. "It's getting late, and I really need to go. You should come too, Emily."

"Great idea. Walk me home?"

They headed for the door. A little voice from the corner of the room tried to stop them. Kate's voice.

"No, guys… Wait—"

"You can come with us."

"You *should* come with us," Emily corrected. "This guy isn't worth your time. You can stay at my house and we'll have a real Christmas, just us."

The fire crackled. The clock ticked. Kate stared at her shoes as if they held the divine secrets of the universe. Maybe they did. Maybe that was the key to her eternal belief everything would work out in her favor: her boots told the future.

"No one should be alone on Christmas."

"He doesn't care about Christmas," Emily shouted, exasperation written in the creasing lines of her forehead.

"I don't," he agreed.

For the first time since their first fiery conversation on the steps of town hall, Kate's firm grasp on her wide-eyed optimism fractured. It was her turn to yell.

"But I do!" She flinched at her own voice, shock visibly rippling through her body at her own reaction. They stared at her, waiting with slack jaws as she ran a hand through her hair and collected herself.

When she returned to them, she was quiet, but no

less emphatic, and to Clark's surprise, she didn't deliver the end of her declaration to the two lifelong friends currently begging her to spend her favorite holiday together. She spoke to him. "I believe in Christmas, and I don't think anyone should be alone like this. Even you."

She left chills up the back of his neck. She'd said the one thing he didn't want to hear. In the corner of his peripheral vision, Emily visibly deflated. Michael threw an arm over her slumped shoulders before walking her towards the door.

"Okay. We'll see you when we see you, I guess. Merry Christmas."

"Merry Christmas, guys."

They left, like the rest of the Miller's Point crowd, through the swinging kitchen door. Eventually, they'd find themselves either leaving from one of the servant's entrances or through the grand front entryway, but for now, their footsteps echoed in Clark's ears and their absence carved a chasm between him and the woman who stayed behind.

Stayed behind with *him*. Because she didn't want him to feel lonely.

Clark didn't know what to do with that information except hate her for it.

"What is your problem?"

"My problem?" he repeated, incredulous. He thought he'd made his *problem* exceptionally clear when he told her he wanted her out of his house, out of his life...and, yeah, out of his head. She'd only been around for less than a day, and still she consumed him. Clark often heard of people describing themselves as "walled off." They "built their walls" to keep themselves protected and others out. Clark's heart wasn't so much a walled castle as it was a vault in Fort Knox. With every word Kate said, he added another steel lock to the door. No one was going to catch him with his guard down, especially not the one woman who'd managed to get under his skin after twenty-seven years on earth.

"Yeah." She crossed her arms, an indication he'd be seeing no more Miss Nice Elf. "I want to know why you're like this."

"I don't need to explain myself to you. This isn't tragic backstory time."

"I want to understand."

"There's nothing to understand."

"*Something* had to make you this way."

Clark paused. His blood rushed in his ears. He wasn't born this way. Statues like him were carved and sculpted and hardened over many years and many miseries. But he'd never told anyone why he hated this stupid holiday, and he wasn't about to start with Kate Buckner, who'd probably end up feeling sorry for him or kissing him or forcing him to let her into his Fort Knox vault of a heart.

"Some people are just the way they are."

"I don't believe that. No one is born lonely."

He'd given her too much room to breathe. The threat to expose his past, the intrusion into his life... It all added up to an attack he didn't know if he possessed the armaments to defeat. He could just push her away until she backed down.

"Christmas is a time where everyone spends money they don't have on people they don't really care about. Or, in this case, they spend other people's money on people they don't really care about."

"I care about you."

"What?"

"I mean…" She bit her bottom lip. "I care about everyone."

No matter what she said, all he heard was, "I care about you." The revelation plunged him into full-on defensive mode.

"I don't. I care about my company, my family, and my legacy. I don't care about Miller's Point. I don't care about your stupid festival. I don't care about Christmas. And I don't care about you. I said you could stay because I felt bad for you, but now I know…"

She stiffened. She froze. Something snapped behind her liquid-gold eyes. She seemed to consider her options. And then, without reaching for her coat or her scarf or anything belonging to her, really, Kate marched towards the nearest door.

"Where are you going?"

"Why are you even asking? You don't care."

The door slammed behind her. Clark knew he should have felt a rush of joy. He'd won. He'd claimed victory over the invading armies of Miller's Point and their fearless leader. But happiness eluded him. It sprinted in the other direction, leaving him empty.

The sustaining belief in goodness she'd carried all through their time together dimmed.

He'd broken Kate Buckner.

He'd been trying to do it all day, but now that he'd succeeded, he felt nothing but disgust.

Chapter Eight

Kate's first thought, as it always was when things went horribly, horribly wrong (or, to be completely fair, even slightly wrong) was, "How did I screw this up?" If a stranger's high heel broke or the set for the Fezziwig mansion got slightly burned by an errant candle fire or no one could agree on how to fairly split a bill at a restaurant, Kate's immediate reaction always passed go, did not collect two hundred dollars, and zipped straight to self-blame.

She abandoned Woodward House behind her, fully intending to return once she cleared her head. The problem with this entire plot of hers came down to one simple fact: being near him drove her crazy.

Crazy didn't accurately describe it. He just…robbed her of any ability she possessed to take decisive, bold action. Kate's performance reviews with The Christmas Company—both during her time as a volunteer and as an employee—always highlighted her excellent ability to think clearly, no matter the circumstances. During times of crisis or mild inconvenience, she took charge and steered the ship back on course. When she got near Clark, however…she might as well have tried to steer the Titanic through nighttime fog.

He made no sense. He surprised her with peeks of his heart and then tore it away when she stepped closer to get a better look. When he offered to drive them on their Christmas Box deliveries, when he gave Bradley that candy bar… Those actions pointed to something specific, to a truth he either wanted to hide or didn't know he had inside of him at all.

He was secretly a good man. He wanted to open himself up to others. But something—fear or pain or resentment—kept him from doing so.

This entire impossible-to-balance calculation led to Kate trudging through the back forty of Woodward House. Thin bands of frozen rain slapped her cheeks. After less than five minutes exposed to the elements, her bones themselves shivered from the cold. Texas never froze, of course, not properly. Snow happened rarely and people usually took it as a sign of the End of Days. But, on days like today, it did get cold enough for Kate to wonder if she would catch her death just trying to get some fresh air.

The forty acres of land stretched between the faux Victorian manor house and the edge of the hill overlooking Miller's Point upon which that house sat. It stirred Kate with its beauty. The old legend of the original Woodwards always included some storyline about Jedediah Woodward, the founder of the town and the company, who bought this land because his bride-to-be—whom he'd never met—apparently loved to paint. He thought buying her a landscape to explore and inspire her art might endear his unseen bride to him. Apparently, the gesture went over fairly well, seeing as she gave him thirteen children.

As she approached the end of the tree line, where a log bridge crossed over an icy river, Kate gave Annabella Woodward some credit. If a man gifted this land to her, she'd probably give him fifteen children. At least.

Stopping at the river's edge, Kate leaned back against a granite boulder and surveyed the vast landscape around her. The rock was not exactly the most comfortable of recliners. She made do anyway. A view so beautiful deserved to be looked at. She could think of no better place to collect her thoughts. The tall evergreen trees followed the river down to a broad estuary in the distance. Unlike the half-frozen, half-cold spit rain, the river really had frozen over, halting the rushing water with a thin top layer of ice.

In the spring especially, she could understand the appeal of Jedediah Woodward's gift to his wife. In a time before flu medicine, one generally appreciated a warm, leafy landscape more than a cold, wet one. Today, with plenty of cold pills and doctors on hand in town, she enjoyed the view for its resilience. Everything froze. Everything died in winter. But that was all the more reason to flourish and blossom come April. Kate sat on the edge of it all, taking in deep breaths of fresh tree breezes as she reckoned with her failings.

She'd failed him, the man with eyes as cold as this landscape. Something in Clark wanted to come out. She saw the hesitant hope hiding in his distant eyes. So why was he being so cruel to her? What had she done to deserve his devil-may-care attitude? She ran circles around this question, poking and prodding and second-guessing every decision she'd made this morning. Every turn she took led her to another brick wall. Every time she thought she'd grabbed onto an answer, her hands clutched at empty air.

She'd been kind and open and honest with him. Maybe she'd been a bit pushy and he made her heart race when he even glanced at her with his hypnotic green eyes, sure, but overall, she'd done nothing but try to help him.

For the first time in a long time, Kate considered the possibility of someone else's failure. Maybe she hadn't failed him. Maybe nothing she could do would open him up. Emily could be right about him. Maybe he just...wasn't a nice guy. Maybe he'd been cruel to her to get her to leave.

With that horrifying yet liberating thought, the full weight of his insults bayoneted her in the chest. *You don't care about me. I don't care about Christmas. I don't care about you.* She heard them the first time, but blamed herself for their stings. Now, she accepted the full weight of his hatred. It burned her worse than the frostbite she was no doubt getting out here in this rain.

It occurred to her how every thought she had about him might have been the product of projection. She assumed everyone could be made to love Christmas because she loved it. She assumed he had a tragic backstory because she lived through a tragedy. She assumed he liked her because...well, against even her best judgment, she liked him. Sure, he could challenge the Grinch for grumpiness and Scrooge for Greatest Miser of All Time. But weirdly, she almost found it endearing, his little freak-outs any time she introduced something new and exciting into his world. He struggled with the basics of human interaction, but she swore he contained good inside of him.

Maybe she'd misjudged his character. Maybe he had nothing inside of him but hate and lumps of coal. She trudged through the woods to clear her head so she could eventually make her way back to the house with fresh eyes and a clear heart, ready to take on anything he threw at her. Now, she could only remember the words Michael always said when she ran to him for advice. *Sometimes,* he said, *you just gotta know when to quit.*

He said it knowing full well she'd never quit. But today...she considered it.

The crack and crunch of leaves behind her ended the internal debate. Kate spooked at the noise—she didn't think a murderer would ever come to a nice place like Miller's Point, but she'd watched enough

Lifetime movies to know it was at least remotely possible—only to slump back down against her rock when she recognized the intruder. For some reason, the man who couldn't stand the sight of her and didn't care about her at all had tracked her down through the rain.

A cynical shade cast over his sudden appearance. Not literally, of course, as she stared out at the frogs sticking to the iced-over river instead of turning to give him her full attention. Was her being on his property a legal liability for him? Did he want her to sign some kind of injury waiver or something?

"H-hey. You're a fast walker," he said. Sudden arrivals didn't catch her attention, but labored, hard-fought gasping did. She turned her head just enough to survey him out of the corner of her eye. A small, eternally happy part of her almost giggled at the sight. Not only was he red-faced and anxious and bent over his knees to catch his breath, but the children of Miller's Point often pretended to be dragons when their breath puffed in front of their face. Imagining Clark on all fours, feigning a mighty dragon's roar, would've brought a less angry Kate to sidesplitting laughter, but as it was, she built a fence of hurt around her.

On the one hand, she needed him to save the town. And she couldn't leave him alone if she thought he had a chance of finding even a sliver of hope. On the other, she selfishly wanted an apology. Her love of Miller's Point and her belief in the goodness of the human heart would eventually dominate any selfish bone in her body, but for this one moment, she indulged in her own pain.

"Only when I'm running away from something. What are you doing here?"

"You're going to get sick."

"You don't care."

"You're still on my employee insurance until January 1."

"Good to know."

A pause. Kate didn't know what he expected by coming down here, and she didn't know what she expected him to say. She knew what she wanted him to say, but she couldn't imagine the words *I'm sorry* ever escaping his lips.

He circled her stone to stand before her, trying to force her to look at him. "Listen—"

"I listened to you all day. I listened to you trash and run over everything I tried to do to make you happy."

"You don't owe me anything. You don't need to make me happy."

"You don't get it, do you? It's not about you. It's about humanity."

"Great. Another soapbox speech about the magical healing powers of Christmas?"

"No. I won't waste it on someone who refuses to listen."

Kate kicked a pebble. It skidded along the dead grass down to the river, where it limply slid across the cracked-ice face of the still water. So, this was defeat. She'd worked so hard to avoid it, she hardly recognized the emotion. Defeat was wanting to scream the truth at the top of her lungs only to have him shove his fingers in his ears and refuse to listen. Defeat was standing in the rain and having someone else tell you it's perfectly dry.

He didn't get her, and she didn't get him. Defeat.

"I hear you." Despite the frost and the perfect cleanliness of his suit, Clark lowered himself to the grass. She couldn't escape his Ireland eyes and their self-serious absurdities. "I'm listening. It's just not for me."

"Christmas is for everyone," she said, for what felt like the millionth time since his arrival here.

"No, it's not."

"But it can be. Christmas is a spirit. Christmas is a way of treating people."

This was perhaps Kate's most deeply held idea about the holiday season. Christmas was there to celebrate the birth of Christ, of course. The name said as much, but because of that, not in spite of it, Christmas had to also embody all of the goodness of humanity. Christmas wasn't just about saying "God bless," but about going out into the world and living that message no matter the personal cost. The only way to truly celebrate Christmas, as far as Kate was concerned, was to stand up for people and love them completely...even if they hurt her.

"Kate..." Clark trailed off and suddenly forgot

how to make eye contact. His big hands must have been very interesting, considering he wouldn't stop staring at them. "I think you're an..." He coughed. "I think you're an extraordinary woman."

"What?"

"You are kind and generous to a fault, even if you were generous with my money—"

"I only spent your money on you."

"You're funny and beautiful and witty and you clearly care about others and—"

He went on, but she stopped listening after beautiful. He thought she was beautiful? Even she didn't think she was beautiful. She tuned back in only after her ears stopped ringing.

"I can see what you're trying to do. I know you're just trying to help. It's a very kind gesture. I just don't want it. I have rules and standards for my life and they just don't include Christmas. Or wasting money. So, I think it would be better if you just go on ahead to your friends' place for Christmas. You'll have a better time."

Kate had only played dodgeball once in her life. This conversation reminded her of being the only person on one side while a barrage attack came from the other. He'd told her, in his stilted Mr. Darcy way, that he liked her, then immediately proceeded into why she needed to spend her holidays without him.

And he'd called her beautiful. His stream of consciousness declaration came out nervous and unfiltered. Had he even realized he called her that?

She changed the subject, if only to keep her heart from exploding with the possibilities. This time, she didn't attack him. A sigh, heavier than any winter wind, blew out of her, releasing the anger and hurt. Clark hadn't managed to say sorry, but he would. She believed in him. Besides, she didn't know how to hold onto anger. It wasn't in her character.

"You know, they're right. I've never left someone alone on Christmas."

"You probably bring them to the festival, don't you?"

"Not always." Kate took a chance. Clark hadn't responded to grand acts of magic or her charming personality. All she had left was her honesty. "Once, when I was eighteen, I'd finally gotten the part of Belle. She's Scrooge's love interest when he's younger. I'd always wanted to play her. She has this beautiful gown and she's just awesome, standing up for herself and breaking up with him when he's not good for her anymore—"

"You like her because she broke up with him?"

"It would have been easy to live with something bad. It took courage to break free and start over."

"I see."

He wasn't convinced, but she pressed forward. In her opinion, he could learn a thing or two from Belle.

"Anyway, this was the only time I was going to be able to play her. I was getting too tall for the costume. I only barely fit into it that year as it was..." She sighed again. "And then Michael broke his leg in the big State Championship football game our senior year of high school. He was going to just stay home that year by himself while everyone went to the festival on Christmas Eve because his parents were working there, but..."

"No one should be alone on Christmas," Clark finished for her.

"Yeah."

"You gave up your big dream just for him?"

Kate scoffed and rolled her eyes.

"My big dream is playing Scrooge. But unless I start growing a beard and some other chromosomes, I don't think that's going to happen."

"You know what I mean. You sacrificed for him."

"Yeah, I guess I did."

"Like you're sacrificing for me."

A clear delineation of thought erupted between them. Kate didn't see it as making a sacrifice. She understood she'd made a sacrifice, but she didn't see it that way or remember it that way. Like tonight, for example, she couldn't imagine ever looking back on it as, "that one Christmas I let a mean guy sneer and yell at me all day." She imagined she'd remember it as, "the year I helped save the town and the soul of a handsome but lonely man with a hidden heart of gold." In the same way, she remembered her eighteenth Christmas as the one where she and Michael played Go Fish until midnight and watched *The Muppet Christmas Carol* on repeat until four in the morning when they both fell asleep on the couch. She woke up with swollen feet because she'd slept in her shoes. She remembered laughing until her sides hurt and eating so much frozen pizza covered in turkey she almost threw up.

Instead of letting him in on this secret, she chose instead to tease him. She liked teasing him. The tops of his ears always turned bright red, a fact that tickled her and made her wonder how many people in his life ever had the guts to make jokes at his expense.

"It's not the same thing."

"Why not?" He furrowed his brow.

"Because I actually sort of like Michael." She shrugged. "Jury's still out on you."

"You don't like me?"

Kate didn't think of herself as a vengeful person, but she internally cheered at the hurt in his voice. It lasted only for a moment before she thoroughly hated herself for it. He'd hurt her when he said he didn't care about her. Part of her wanted him to hurt, however horrible that desire was.

"Have you done anything to make me like you?"

"Well…" He stumbled. "I mean…"

"Uh-huh," Kate retorted, triumphantly, happy to have a reason to smile again. She'd been frowning for too long. "So, why would I like you if you haven't done anything to earn it?"

"I can be nice."

"Yeah?"

"Yeah."

They sat in unmoving silence for one minute. Then two minutes. All the while, Kate stared. When he finally got uncomfortable with her gaze, he raised his eyebrows in confusion.

"What?"

"I'm waiting," Kate said, unable to help chuckling.

"Waiting on what?"

"For you to be nice!"

Clark joined her laughter. Not much. Not enough. But it was a start.

"Why don't we call a truce? A real one this time," he said, the ghost of a smile still pulling at his lips. "You can have your Christmas, and I'll have my peace and quiet in my study."

"My Christmas is the festival. Are you going to give me that?"

"No."

"But—"

The smile vanished. Clark's right hand flexed.

"We can't call a truce if you're going to be impossible."

"I am not being impossible!"

"You know I'm not going to give you the festival back. We can't afford it."

Here we go again, Kate thought. *Two steps forward, one step back.*

"That's not why we can't have it."

"It's a drain on our resources."

"Maybe, but that's not the real reason you're shutting it down," she retorted.

"Are we really going through this dance again?"

"I'll do it until you tell me what you've got against Christmas."

"You'll be dancing forever, then."

Kate explored two distinct possibilities laid out before her. Either he was a snob who would never attempt to open himself up to her or anyone else, for that matter—a possibility she found remote now that he admitted to liking her, something he never would have this morning—or he was going to flourish into the man she thought he could be. The man she saw hiding behind his thick curtains of cold detachment. Either way, she had to keep trying. The town hung in the balance and a man's soul was at stake. This was no time to hide at Emily's house and drink eggnog until she passed out, even if she wanted to.

"Why don't I make you a deal? Instead of hiding in your office like the saddest man in the world, you spend Christmas with me. Really with me. Not on your phone pretending I don't exist. And if you still hate it tomorrow morning, you don't have to tell me why. But if you like it, even a little bit, you have to fess up."

She wanted that secret. Knowing it could be the change in everything. It could make the difference.

"...Why do I have a feeling you won't take no for an answer?"

"Because I won't." She smiled and popped up from her rock. The cracked face of her childhood Mickey Mouse watch flashed in the dim light peeking from behind the towering fir trees. Already five o'clock?

When had it gotten so late? There were so many Christmas Eve traditions to get through before the evening was out. Her mind raced with timetables and planning strategies as her boots crunched the frosty grass beneath her feet. The slight shower still trickled overhead, but she paid it no mind; they'd be warm enough once they made it inside and in front of a roaring fireplace. She rubbed her hands together to warm them, not considering the fact that she might look like a plotting, evil supervillain.

"Then I guess I accept your deal."

All at once, Kate bloomed into her normal self. It was Christmas. Anything could happen at Christmas. And what was more, she was *great* at Christmas. Renewed faith squeezed her chest.

"Then you'd better get ready for the best Christmas of your life," she commanded.

"That's an incredibly low bar to clear."

"Then you'd better get ready for the best Christmas of all time."

"You haven't convinced me so far." He smirked. "I accept your challenge."

Chapter Nine

H e accepted her deal only because he convinced himself it was impossible to falter. He would never like Christmas, and even if she did make him enjoy it a little bit, he could just lie and save himself the humiliation of telling his story.

And besides, he was a businessman. He didn't respect any deal not in writing.

When she fled the house, he had no choice but to go after her. Reason told him he couldn't let a woman wander around outside alone, especially not on his property. Reason told him she'd gone outside without a coat or an umbrella. She'd catch her death! She'd slip on the ice and fall and break her neck! She'd see a stray lightbulb and electrocute herself trying to fix it!

Reason instilled him with a sense of fear for her safety, but reason, if he ever decided to be honest with himself, only served as a justification for stepping out into the biting rain and following her footprints through the wet grass into the forest. As a kid, these woods had terrified him. He hadn't stepped foot past the treeline since his ninth birthday. Twenty years later, these woods still featured in some of his worst nightmares.

But he'd forged ahead anyway. Kate couldn't be out in the woods alone, not when he had been the one to push her out there.

Clark didn't have the time or patience for feelings like guilt. At least, he didn't until he met Kate. She was the human face behind his corporate destruction, and even if he still believed he was doing the right thing, she made him want to apologize. She made him wish there was another way.

So, that's why he said what he did about her, about her being kind and good-hearted. She needed to know this wasn't personal. She hadn't failed him. He just didn't buy into her gimmicks about the holiday season, that's all.

"We might as well get it over and done with," he said, picking himself up from the muddy forest floor. Usually, he preferred clean, Scandinavian office design to dirt and outdoors of any kind, but he made an exception for Kate.

"No need to sound so excited," she teased.

"I don't want this deal going to your head."

"Don't worry. I'm under no illusions you'll be an easy nut to crack."

"Good."

"But you shouldn't let this deal go to your head, either."

"Why?"

She spun on him, her long hair whipping waves of cinnamon and evergreen-scented air Clark's way. It stunned him as she leaned in close, too close for comfort. Not that he minded. With her this close and this mockingly intense, he could count the millions of near-gold flecks in her eyes and feel her puffing breath on his lips.

"Because you'll find I'm a very persistent gal."

"I already know that," he whispered, too low for her to hear, a fact he was grateful for. If she heard him, she might discover that *I already know that* was code for something else, an electric hum that stirred inside him every time she said his name.

Unfazed, she stretched her arms out. Arms open wide as if to hug the scenery around her, she tilted her head back and breathed. This place held nothing but anxiety and headaches for Clark, but Kate was perfectly at peace. Out here, away from the distractions of the Christmas lights and the electric bill no doubt climbing, he beheld her. Every soft curve of her beautiful face glowed against this frigid terrain. She smiled even as frozen raindrops slid down her skin. A cold would no doubt be in both of their futures if Clark didn't usher them back to the house soon.

A cold seemed a small price to pay to get to see Kate like this, surrounded by silver rain falling down in thin sheets against the emeralds and ambers of the woods towering around them. Set against this backdrop, she reminded him of a princess in a fairy story, one raised so deep in the forest she didn't even know she was royalty.

"This place is beautiful, isn't it?" she asked.

"Yeah," he breathed, never once glancing at the scenery. He was too wrapped up in her. "I guess it is."

"You guess? Don't you know?"

"I don't like these woods. Haven't since I was a kid. I got lost in them once."

The memories of that day still haunted him. He prayed she wouldn't pry.

"And..." She trailed off, her eyes narrowing in cautious suspicion, "you still came out to look for me?"

"It was the logical thing to do."

It wasn't *only* logical, but Kate didn't push. In the fashion of a distracted hummingbird, Kate broke the tenuous emotional connection between them. She changed the subject with surprising deftness, adopting a half-bent pose to examine his feet.

"What're your shoes like?"

"What?" An unapproved laugh escaped. How had he gotten from wanting to sweep her into his arms and kiss her in the middle of a drizzle to being asked about the quality of his shoes?

"Let me have a look at them," she demanded, bending down even further to pick up one of his legs. Clark gripped the nearest tree for support when his left leg was hoisted unceremoniously in the air. If Kate were any other woman, if this were any other day, and if he hadn't struck that deal, fury would have ruled him.

It was, however much he resented it, Christmas Eve. He did make a deal. And the woman holding his leg in the air was Kate, this strange, smiley, fireplace of a woman who weaseled her way behind his defenses.

"Why do you need to look at my shoes?"

She dropped his left leg and reached for his right. A sudden wave of embarrassment gripped Clark by the scruff of the neck, digging cold, sharp nails into the skin beneath his hairline. These shoes were—he mentally counted backwards—about twenty years old. He'd watched countless YouTube tutorials on cobbling so he could fix them up and keep them instead of spending a few hundred bucks on a new pair. Besides, they were his father's shoes. He didn't want to just throw them away. Could she tell they were holding together with shoe glue and a prayer?

"I need to make sure they've got enough grip on them."

"Okay. Wait, grip on them for what?"

Clunk. His right leg hit the ground, returning him to even footing. Kate rose, her cheeks flushed from the weather and whatever excitement bubbled behind that skull of hers. Having spent approximately zero time out in freezing rain before, the pink tint of her skin concerned him. His obliging attitude was going to land both of them in the hospital with a horrible flu or something.

Though he couldn't deny, at least to himself, how beautiful she was. With her hair now damp from the rain and her clothes sticking to her skin, a woman who should have looked like a drowned cat ended up glowing in the hazy sunlight like a beached siren. She kicked her own shoes against the nearest tree trunk, knocking out clumps of dirt and mud from between the treads. Her pink cheeks and nose belonged on a romantic Christmas card. Clark's confusion only grew.

"Are you up for an adventure?" she asked.

"Uh…" As much as he relished the golden thrill streaking through her gaze, he didn't like the sound of the word *adventure* on her red lips. "Not really. Why do you ask?"

Once again, Kate opened her arms to the scenery, only this time she didn't relish it or show it off. Clark followed her gaze out into the clearing before them. It was only now, with his attention fully focused on it, he realized this wasn't a clearing at all.

They'd reached the river.

"There's a family of cardinals across the water. Can you hear them?"

"Yes, but—"

"When I was a kid, one of my teachers used to hand-paint these Christmas cards with cardinals in snowy trees. We don't get snow here, but we've got to see if we can spot them."

Oh, no. Her voice recovered its bell-like ring, the same bell-like ring it got every time she wasn't going to take no for an answer. A snake of panic slithered down Clark's spine as she inched towards the long log bridge connecting the two banks of the still river; in less than a second, his anxious mind conjured up a list of at least twenty-eight things that could go wrong. He grasped at any reason not to follow through with this scheme.

"Don't you have a zoo around here? A bird sanctuary or something? You can see cardinals anytime."

"Oh, please," Kate scoffed and peeled off her now properly wet overcoat. It landed with a *splat* on her lounging rock. "Why would I go to a zoo when there's a perfectly good nest across the river?" When she sensed his hesitation, she sighed and extended her hand, her energy very much projecting a *just shut up and have fun for once in your life* vibe. "It'll be fun."

"That bridge isn't up to code."

"They're big old logs. It's probably been there for a hundred years. What more do you want?"

He pressed his back into the nearest tree. If wishes came true, the massive trunk would open up and swallow him whole. No such salvation came. He cursed this stupid forest; no wonder he hadn't come in here for almost twenty years. All the trees were jerks.

"Nope. No way." He shook his head, hoping his stern voice would be enough to indicate that he was putting his foot down about this one. He'd given her run of his house, his car, and his kitchen, but he really meant it this time when he said no. "It's not safe. Kate—"

Pleas fell on deaf ears as the woman in question took a challenging step forward, slapping her heeled boot onto the bark of the makeshift bridge. Clark's steady heartbeat picked up tempo and volume until it sounded like an overexcited drumline had taken a residency in his ears.

"You know you want to..."

Another step forward. Both of her feet were on the log now, only a foot or two above the iced-over water, but enough to worry him. Her smile curled upward. She thought she had the upper hand; she believed he would follow her straight out over the river, bending to her will. Clark's fear kept him rooted to the spot even as his heart pounded against the cage of his chest, trying to escape and run straight for her. Across the river, the song of the cardinals—he assumed they were cardinals, at least—taunted him.

"I don't—"

Another step. She spread her arms out for balance.

"You're going to miss all the fun," she promised in a singsong cadence.

"You're going to be cold," he countered.

Another step. The heel of her boot narrowly missed a gap in the wood and his heart narrowly missed two beats. Her steps were small, cautious, and though she no longer looked at him, he would be willing to bet his fortune that she was smirking.

"You sure you don't want to join me?"

"Hey," Clark warned, this time moving forward in step with her. He kept his hands out in front of him in a show of surrender. Approaching her as if she were a wounded animal, he mentally begged her not to move another muscle.

"Just a little bit closer..." She crooned.

Clark halted in place. So *that* was her game. Trickery. He was *not* going to cross those logs. Games and sneaking around wouldn't work anymore than bribery or pleading would. Instead, he turned away from the river and headed for the path straight home.

He wasn't actually going to go home, of course. He just needed her to think he was so she would be inclined to follow him. Two could play at her game.

"I'm not doing this. You won't pressure me."

His reverse psychology failed. A huff from behind him told him so.

"Fine! I'll just go by my—"

A crack. A piercing scream. A rush of water. Three sounds wrapped up in one cymbal crash of noise. Clark spun on his heel.

"Kate! KATE!"

But Kate was gone. She'd fallen. Broken the ice sheet. And the river—still only a second ago—now rushed away from him. Taking Kate with it.

He didn't think twice. He didn't have to. His body acted for him. Without a moment's hesitation, his powerful legs crossed the muddy ground and he dove head-first into the frigid water. It stung, a million frozen daggers cutting into his skin.

He crashed beneath the surface. His eyes opened, but the water was so black and cold he could neither see anything nor feel anything but pain. Slamming them closed again, he stretched his arm out before him. Once. Twice. His body shoved the water aside, searching for the one thing he needed to save. His lungs ached for air. His skin screamed from the cold. Currents pulled him, dragging him away, but he urged his muscles forward. He opened his eyes once, then twice, but besides the stinging this action caused him, he couldn't see a thing. He was swimming blindly, praying with every motion that he'd somehow find her. He *had* to find her.

Finally, his hand touched something warm and solid. Or, he tried to. Her body revolted against him, thrashing and shoving wildly as she fought to struggle towards the air above them. Gripping her by the waist, he swam upward, fighting with strained muscles to struggle against the punishing current. Everything was cold. Everything was painful. But he couldn't dwell. Thought vanished, leaving only the primal. It shoved him onward even when he wanted nothing more than to quit. *Survive. Save her and survive.* But with each passing second, her body grew more and more limp, and she fought less and less...until one cruel moment when she went still and slack in his arms.

"Ah!" He gasped when they finally hit the air. He drank it in, coughing and choking and spluttering. Kate returned to life, too, though not as violently as he. As he pushed their way crosscurrent to the river's dirty bank, Clark watched Kate's limp head barely suck in air. Her entire body shook with shivers, but at least she was breathing. Her eyes fluttered enough to tell him she was conscious. A small, desperate relief.

Clark moved quickly. They needed to get back inside. No time to waste, not when he'd been so supremely stupid. Every second they wasted not moving towards the house was a moment she wasn't getting the care she needed. Wordless and shivering himself, Clark scooped Kate into his arms, bridal style, and set his eyes on the peak of the house poking out from just over the trees in the distance. They left the clearing and the river behind, but not before he picked up Kate's coat, the one she'd discarded before her expedition across the log bridge.

Invisible needles stabbed him as his wet skin met cold air. He could only imagine what Kate was going through. Her now-pale body almost convulsed in his arms, though she kept the slightest of grips on his neck. The pressure provided him a small modicum of relief. As long as she touched him, he knew she wasn't under.

The forest that scared him so deeply as a child now served as mere window dressing. Nothing mattered but getting her home. As he walked, he tried to keep her awake. What little warmth he felt in her body slipped away with every step he took.

"All right, Kate. It's all right. We're gonna get you home and take care of you. I promise. I just need you to stay awake and stick with me, okay?" he muttered incoherently, not that it mattered. The words weren't important. He spoke to give her something to hold onto...and to keep his mind off of the fact that he let her get hurt. She could freeze to death or get hypothermia or lose her legs and it would be all his fault. All because he didn't want to sit around a warm fire and sing Christmas songs.

With one hand, Clark maneuvered the coat his hands until he was able to pull out the cell phone from her pocket.

"Kate, what's your password?"

"No password," she mumbled, her head curling into the space between Clark's shoulder and neck. Her breath tickled. At least it hadn't lost its heat yet. Her phone lit his face, clearly asking for a password. Did she not want to give it to him, or was she so out of it she thought she didn't have one? Clark racked his brain. He couldn't stop his walking and he needed help. He couldn't help her alone.

Then it came to him. And he pressed four numbers. They granted him access. 1-2-2-5. December 25. Christmas Day. She really *did* love Christmas as much as she claimed. During their tour yesterday, Michael informed him that the nearest hospital was in the next town over, meaning even the fastest ambulance would be miles behind someone who lived in town. They'd never make it in time to save Kate. He needed someone who could help. And he needed them fast. Making quick work of the damp phone screen, he clicked the first name he recognized. The voice on the other end of the line answered in one ring.

"I knew you'd come around! Want me and Michael to pick you up—"

"Do you know a doctor?"

"What? Who is this?"

"Emily, there's been an accident. Kate needs—"

"Woodward? Is that you?"

"Kate fell into the river trying to cross this log bridge and she needs to see a doctor."

"Is it serious?"

"I don't know, but I need your help."

"Michael's a medic."

"Come to the house as quick as you can." She didn't respond. Desperation coursed through him. "*Please*."

"We'll be there in ten."

Clark could only hope ten minutes would be fast enough. Michael's medical expertise was their only hope. He hung up and continued his journey.

When the tree line broke, Woodward House loomed into view. Clark, who had until now been walking as fast as his legs would allow, pulled into a dead sprint. Kate's hold on his shoulders had loosened. He was losing her to unconsciousness. Terror replaced his blood. The color evaporated from his world. He pressed onward into the house and upstairs to the first bathroom he could find. Shoving open the door with his shoulder, he entered and placed Kate on the counter, letting her body slacken against the wall. Her eyes slipped closed. They no longer fluttered. Clark fought the urge to vomit.

"Hey, hey, I need you to listen to me." He tapped her hand, perhaps a little harder than necessary. It twitched, a good response. As he continued to speak, Clark spun the bathtub faucet. A small chain—part of the ancient plumbing system in this house—needed to be pulled for the shower, but as the water heated up, Clark reached for the nearest towel and tried to figure out what to do next as he frantically rubbed the barely-conscious woman dry. He couldn't leave Kate in the shower alone. She'd drown. Waiting for Michael the medic would take too long. Kate needed warmth now.

With great care, Clark lifted Kate off of the counter, carried her to the steaming shower, and stepped inside with her, fully clothed.

The shower, like the rest of the house, showed its age. Glass and gold couldn't have been more out of fashion; the pipes groaned from the sudden use of the hot water. Clark only saw the woman in his arms. He placed her on her own two feet, but held her close, almost as if they were dancing. The hot water washed over them in a steaming, restorative rain storm. *Please be all right*, he silently begged her. *Please, please, please be all right.* He counted her heartbeats against his chest, marking each one as a victory, a sign she could make it through this.

Slowly, Kate's chattering teeth stilled. Her body ceased its convulsions. She looked up at Clark with an expression of half-awake awe, her heart hammering against his chest.

"You..." She trailed off. "You..."

Clark wanted to pull the rest of the words from her mind. What was she trying to say? Did she hate him for letting her fall down through the ice or love him for bringing her back or despise him for standing in the shower with her, even if they were fully clothed?

He would never find out. The bathroom door slammed open, revealing a red-faced Emily. Steam practically shot out of her ears, though Michael followed behind with level-headed stoicism.

"You!" Emily's voice ricocheted off the tiled bathroom walls. "What do you think you're doing?"

"I'm trying to help her."

"Help her? I think you've done enough. Now, go."

A protest shoved its way to the front of Clark's brain. He abandoned all thoughts of confrontation. As much as he hated to admit it, Emily was right. He put Kate in a terrible position and let her fall. If he stayed, the chances of him screwing it up even further only grew.

"Of course. Thank you for coming to help."

Awkwardly, he changed places with Emily. He walked his soaking wet body straight out of the bathroom and past Michael, without another word. The only thing he could do now was get himself cleaned up and wait.

About twenty minutes, a shower and a fresh set of clothes later, Clark found himself pacing outside of her bathroom door. He heard no sound, but it didn't deter him. He'd wait as long as he needed to see her, to make sure she was all right.

He didn't know how long he paced before a door down the hallway opened, revealing Emily. She hugged an oversized sweater to her chest.

"Is Kate all right?"

"She's fine. I borrowed some old pajamas from a drawer and put her to bed. Is that okay?" When Clark nodded, Emily glanced over her shoulder to make sure the bedroom door from which she emerged remained closed before leveling her uncertain expression at him. "Listen. I gotta talk to you."

"Yes?"

"I don't like you. I mean…" She rolled her eyes. A sigh blew rough between her lips. "I *didn't* like you. But Kate said you saved her from the river, is that true?"

Save. Clark knew how to destroy things. Subsidiaries and businesses. He knew how to dismantle them and sell off the parts. He wasn't sure he was comfortable being described as a man who saved anything, much less a woman's life. Much less *Kate's* life. He wasn't worthy of the distinction.

"She fell and I went in to get her," he said, diplomatically.

"And carried her all the way here and did everything you could to make sure she was all right?"

Clark merely nodded. Slumping back against the nearest wall, and disturbing an ancient painting of Clark's third great uncle Horace in the process, Emily released a long, low sigh of contradiction, not that Clark blamed her. He'd ridden into town, insulted everyone she knew, and gotten her friend almost killed. Him saving her life didn't change or negate the other facts of their interactions. But he did save her life.

"I can't believe I'm saying this, but thank you. Kate sees something in you I just don't. But I'm glad she was right."

"What does she see in me?"

"…She sees a good man somewhere inside of you. I thought she was crazy, but maybe she's onto something. She's got a good eye for that sort of thing."

It went entirely without saying that Emily thought Kate's idea of Clark as a good man didn't hold up to much scrutiny. He could accept that. He hadn't exactly been a good friend to anyone in this town; he deserved their ire, at least where Kate was concerned. Everyone here held her in such high regard. If he failed her, he failed the town. If he saved her, they didn't mind him quite so much. Before he could respond, Michael emerged from the door, backpack haphazardly slung over his shoulder.

"How is she? Can I see her?" Clark asked.

It was one thing to know someone was all right and quite another to see them with his own two eyes. Kate's cold, unresponsive body haunted him; her smile could cure the sickening fear humming beneath his skin.

"I think we should let her sleep. She isn't hypothermic, thanks to your help, but she needs to stay warm and rest. She needs a little bit of peace and quiet after everything she's been through today."

"Okay. Thank you." An idea, a tentative, hesitant idea but an idea nonetheless. "Do you want to stay for Christmas?"

The pair shared a wary look.

"I'll drop by tomorrow," Emily said. "We have some things to take care of in town." They started to depart, but she stopped and turned before she went. "But thank you."

Since arriving in Miller's Point, Clark couldn't think of anyone thanking him. They hated him. Made snarky comments behind his back. Criticized Kate for spending time with him. No one ever thanked him until that moment.

As it turned out, he enjoyed being liked more than he enjoyed being hated.

Chapter Ten

Kate didn't know what Michael put in that hot chocolate, but it must have been stronger than morphine and tasteless as water. One minute, she shivered under the covers and warmed her hands against the walls of the steaming mug; the next, she woke from a dream (where she starred as an animated Who in one of those Grinch movies) with a slight start. As she blinked against the darkness, it took her a moment to remember where she was and what had happened. The bedroom, with its crackling fireplace and slightly dusty fixtures—no one had been in here but the caretaker for almost a year now—engulfed her with its largeness. Kate cocooned herself in the warm covers, feeling more than a bit like Alice in Wonderland after downing the shrinking potion. Her entire apartment could fit in this one bedroom.

Against her better judgment, she had to wonder: how could a guy with a house like this be worried about money? Clark was, to put it mildly, a complete and total miser. A penny-pincher. The festival was just the visible tip of the iceberg. She'd even caught a glimpse into his car's trunk during their trip to bring food to the families on the outskirts of town. He claimed he intended to spend one week in town, but only packed one backpack's worth of clothes. Everything about him proclaimed his truth: money mattered, and he wasn't going to waste a penny of it, even if those pennies might make an entire community happy.

He had everything. But more than everything, he had nothing. Nothing of any value. Kate didn't have a lot—she worked for the festival because she loved it, not because the festival was paying her well—but even though she counted pennies and cut coupons so she could work in her dream job, richness filled her life. Emptiness filled Clark's.

Her heart bled for him.

"No," she muttered. "No more sitting around."

Admittedly, she struggled to make her heavy limbs rip the covers away and expose her body to the cold air of the old house, but she couldn't stay in bed any longer. Her eyes flickered to the clock above the mantel. Eight o'clock. Eight o'clock gave her... She counted on her fingers... Twenty-eight hours until the end of Christmas altogether. Twenty-eight hours to change a life, to fill it to the brim with magic.

Slipping out of bed, she marveled at the soft slouch of the pajama material against her skin. It served as a good distraction against the cold floor beneath her feet. It should figure Clark would have a massive, historical house with every modern luxury only to ignore the modern amenities like under-floor heating in favor of lighting a sooty fireplace.

As Kate crossed the room, she caught her own reflection in the mirror. Her makeup came off in the wash, her hair remained damp after her shower, and the pajamas Emily dug up from one of the wardrobes weren't the traditional Christmas pajamas she always wore because those were tucked in her overnight bag, which was subsequently shoved into a random closet on the first floor as Emily was in a rush to get her into bed.

Emily. Kate paused at the door. Before slipping into the oblivion of a Seuss-themed dream, Emily gave her explicit instructions not to get out of bed until Christmas morning, citing Kate-cicle's need to warm her bones and recover with some sleep. Kate cracked the oaken bedroom door slightly.

"Emily?" she called.

The house breathed in response, but no answer made its way through the halls. She cleared her throat, raising her voice lightly.

"Emily? Are you out there?"

Kate wanted to pretend her friend's protective, fiery nature didn't scare her, but that would have been a lie. This quiet, cautious check if the coast was clear was the only thing separating her from Emily's anger at being disobeyed. Kate counted to five. Then, to ten. When no voice or heavy footsteps answered, she took her first brave steps into the belly of the darkened house.

The darkness chilled Kate at first; it chilled her almost as deep as the frozen water. It pierced her skin. It amplified every creaking floorboard beneath her feet. Like a heroine in a gothic romance, she pressed on. Clark Woodward was somewhere in this house. She only needed to find him.

But finding him meant first finding a light. Any light. Kate groped around the pitch-black hallway, searching for a cord. Just this morning she did all of the wiring for the strung lights down this hallway. If she could only find the plug...

"There!"

Kate pressed the metal tongs into the outlet and the hallway burst back to carnival-like life. A sigh of relief escaped her. Clark had been miserly enough to turn off all the lights before 9 p.m. on Christmas Eve, but at least he hadn't taken them all down.

Guided by her new light, Kate pressed onward. Clark would be around here somewhere...she just had to find him.

The voices in Clark's head wouldn't stop yammering. For the past two hours, they argued and debated, sparred and grappled like two prize fighters trying to go the distance.

You should go check on her.

Emily said to leave her alone.

But it's Christmas and she's missing it.

You don't care about Christmas.

No, but she does… Maybe she'll be upset if you let her sleep through it.

If you wake her up, she'll probably be sick and then you'll have to put up with her making you do all of her tradition stuff all night.

…That might not be so bad.

Who are you and what have you done with Clark Woodward?

Christmas is pointless, sure. Wasteful and stupid, of course. But today's been the best Christmas I've had in a long time.

A woman almost died on your watch.

My comment still stands. Best Christmas since I was a kid.

That's an awfully low bar to clear.

I should go check on her.

She doesn't want to see you.

For two hours, it went on like that, all while he attempted to get some semblance of work done. With the office in Dallas closed after five o'clock and everyone home for the holiday here in Miller's Point, he had no one to do business *with*, but he still found paperwork to read and files to sort through. About an hour into his mental torture, he'd shifted from a secretarial office to his uncle's actual office, hoping to find more busywork there. It was eerie, being in a dead man's office, almost as strange as being in a dead family's house. Except for a few distant cousins, only Clark remained of the Woodward clan. He was the last of his kind, in a way. It made the wall of family photos lining his uncle's office all the more difficult to bear. Burying his head in the nearest drawer to avoid looking at them, Clark picked up stacks of paper at random and began sorting them. Busywork though it was, at least it was distracting busywork. His uncle had been many things, but a brilliant organizational mind, he most certainly was not.

Clark stacked papers into piles by subject matter, then date. When he'd accomplished that, he sorted by last name of the signatory partner, then date. He shuffled and re-shuffled and tried to get it into an appropriate filing system until finally realizing the filing system wasn't the problem.

He was worried about Kate. Not in the "she's a woman in my house and I need to make sure she's safe because that's what a good host does" way. Not in a detached gentlemanly way.

The longer she remained out of sight, the more he realized how wrong he was when he said "I don't care about you." He hardly knew her, but he cared about her. There was no getting around it or denying it.

Only one thing remained unclear: what to do about it. Caring meant investment. Caring meant friendship. For all he knew…if he spent more time here…caring could mean even more than friendship. Caring meant giving her things he didn't know he could give.

No. No. He couldn't do it. He'd just have to…lock

himself in here until she gave up and abandoned him. It was the only way to move on. Maybe he was getting ill. Being sick always made him think crazy things. Maybe she bewitched him or something. Small towns usually had a witch, if made-for-TV movies had any truth to them. In any case, he couldn't be allowed to care for her. He'd just have to hide himself away until she shrunk and took up less and less room in his small, used-up heart.

After a day spent in this massive mansion, Kate assumed her hold on the geography of the place was pretty strong. Unfortunately, the house took on a life of its own after dark. Every gothic romance she read said as much, but she didn't believe it until she wandered the halls of Woodward House without a clue how to get around. This house needed a "You Are Here" map...or a logical layout. Whenever Kate thought she'd figured out where she was, she turned into what she *thought* was the living room, only to find she'd stumbled upon an indoor squash court or a stadium-sized library. Like a real-life episode of Scooby-Doo, she would enter a door and seem to come out halfway across the house. She didn't believe in curses or hauntings or anything so ridiculous, but if any house in the world was going to be under a spell, the old house on the hill of Miller's Point was probably the most likely of candidates.

It seemed to go on like that for hours, until she

finally stumbled upon the staircase leading down to the first floor. Tripping down the stairs in her excitement, Kate rushed for the living room, practically slipping in her socks as she slid towards the living room and tossed open the doors.

"Hey, Clark!"

…she said, to an entirely empty, darkened room. A flick of the light switch revealed this was no prank. He just wasn't there.

Kate's stomach grumbled. Going to the kitchen would kill two birds with one stone; she'd have her fill of whatever she could find in the fridge, and the resonant noise from her singing against the tile floors and backsplash would carry easily to wherever Clark hid in this massive manor.

She waltzed through the swinging door. The kitchen was not as she left it this morning, hustling and bustling with overflowing platters and saucepans. Its tidiness smacked of Clark's presence. He'd been in here recently, and he'd cleaned the house of any trace of her guests and their feast. Kate's stomach grumbled, more insistently this time.

"Yeah, yeah. I hear you," she muttered, patting her own gut.

To her great relief, cobwebs and canned chickens were not the only thing lining the pantry. Leftover sundries and dishes from the luncheon—left behind by eager-to-leave guests—littered the cupboards and the refrigerator. Sating her hunger temporarily, Kate picked at a honey-roasted ham from the fridge as she explored the rest of her options. *Sweet potato biscuits... Apple pie... Garlic mashed potatoes... Roasted cauliflower... Turkey legs... Stuffed artichokes.*

When she opened the fridge, all debate ceased. Trays of frozen sugar cookie dough waited to be cut out and baked to golden, sugary perfection. A devious smile painted itself across Kate's hungry lips.

"Come to Mama..."

Clark's mental takedown of his errant flicker of emotion for Kate effectively ceased the worried voice in his head, finally giving him the clarity to properly order his files. First by department, then by date.

He continued on this way for too long before a distraction slithered under the door of the office, infiltrating his space and filling every corner. He couldn't escape it. He couldn't hide from it.

Cookies. Sugar cookies. His one weakness. The one redeeming quality of Christmas, as far as Clark was concerned, was the packets of frozen cookies with the Santa faces and trees pressed colorfully into the top. The smell of those cookies haunted him now, wafting through the walls of this old house like the ghost of a long-forgotten dream.

Leaping to his feet, Clark made it halfway to the door before realizing the dilemma he now found himself in: he could pursue his goal of falling out of like with Kate, or he could see her and have cookies.

The voice speaking for his hidden emotions jumped at the first opportunity to speak again.

If you go downstairs, you can check to see if she's okay and you can have cookies. Kill two birds with one stone.

You'll regret it if you go down there. Wait until she leaves or falls asleep, then go down and get those sweet, sweet cookies.

If you wait, they'll be cold.

Put them in the microwave for ten seconds. Bam! Good as new.

It's not good as new, and you know it.

Is too.

Is-

"God rest ye Merry Gentlemen, let nothing you dismay…"

The voices silenced when one very particular voice reached Clark's ears. The confident tune joined the cookie-scented air in tying a knot around his stomach and pulling him exactly where they wanted him to go. Trapped in the hypnotic pull of her voice and his love of sweets, he left behind his doubts and followed them down into the kitchen.

After all, what was the worst that could happen? It's not like cookies would make him fall in love with her or anything.

Chapter Eleven

After uncovering the frozen sheets of cookie dough resting atop some Tupperware containers of butternut squash soup and tubs of eggnog ice cream, Kate made quick work of baking, and within a few minutes, the marble counters turned snow-white and sticky. Without a cookie-cutter or can of baking spray in sight, she improvised, using a wire star ornament to cut out the dough. A brief dig through the pantry and the fridge rewarded her with flour and butter to grease the cookie sheets. The available dough was meant to feed at least forty people, so once the first batch entered the oven, Kate focused on the next twenty or so cookies.

Did she *need* to bake every single bit of dough left behind in the freezer? Of course not. Even at her most hungry, Kate's cookie-eating record never broke seventeen cookies in a single sitting. The end product of the baking wasn't the point, really. She baked because it gave her something to do, something to occupy her hands as she tried to plan her next steps. The night was still young, and she wasn't sure she'd made any progress with Clark earlier. Sure, he'd been slightly nicer to her than he was this morning, but he hadn't seemed any more sympathetic to Christmas or the cause of saving the festival. She certainly had her work cut out for her. If a redecorated house, a feast and a visit to the river didn't convince him, what would?

"Smells good in here."

The steaming tray of cookies in Kate's hands almost went flying across the room as a voice from the door behind her spooked her straight out of her skin.

"Sorry, sorry! Did I scare you?"

"I don't know." She dropped the steaming plate of cookies onto the counter as her free hand flew to her chest. She could feel her pounding heartbeat. Like being faked out by a horror movie jump-scare, Kate couldn't help but chuckle even as she shivered in fear. "Maybe you should ask my ghost. You can't just sneak up on people like that!"

Clark hovered in the doorway, halfway into the kitchen and halfway out, as if he couldn't decide whether or not to fully engage with her. Since waking to find him precisely nowhere in his own house, Kate assumed Clark had been hiding from her to avoid any more Christmas talk, despite his promise to at least try and enjoy her company. Thinking he hated her and her holiday so much had stung, and his arrival here and now soothed the wounds only slightly. To his credit, Clark gave off a sufficiently sheepish air. He filled the room with his uncertainty.

"I smelled cookies."

Oh. A stab of disappointment shot straight up Kate's arm, following the flow of her blood until it pierced and filled her heart. He hadn't come because he wanted to talk to her or come out of hiding. She'd angered him with more supposed "waste" of his family's resources. Kate turned her back on him. If he wanted to chew her out, fine. But she didn't have to pay attention. She transferred the steaming cookies from the baking sheet to the cooling rack she'd found in the back of a dusty cabinet.

"Don't worry. I didn't spend any of your money to make them."

"No, that's not why I'm here. I just wanted one."

"Really?"

"I like sugar cookies." He shrugged. "Is that a crime?"

"Not at all." If anything, the defensive admission only endeared him to her. Clark prowled around Miller's Point with all of the arrogant attitude of a demigod. Liking cookies made him more human in her eyes. She tried to imagine Clark sitting on a beat-up couch somewhere eating a plate full of cookies for Santa. The picture never came into focus. "It's just surprising, I guess."

"Why?"

"You don't like anything other people like. I just

assumed you usually eat nothing but plain yogurt and protein bars. And water."

Given that he didn't know she'd been accidentally spying on him, she couldn't tell him she'd seen him order a plate of pancakes and bacon at Mel's, so she stuck with gentle teasing instead. As someone who ate almost every breakfast at a greasy diner in the town square, Kate couldn't think of anything more disgusting than plain yogurt and protein bars. She preferred her pancakes like Emily preferred her men: rich and sweet.

"There's nothing wrong with plain yogurt," was his weak defense.

"Yeah, if you enjoy things that don't taste good."

Clark reached for the cookies, stopping himself short in a "where are my manners" way.

"May I?"

"No, I'm sorry. They're all for me."

"You're gonna eat all..." Sweeping the cooling rack with his eyes, Clark gave a quick whispered count under his breath. "All twenty-four of these?"

"I'm hungry."

"Seriously?"

"No, not seriously," she huffed. "Eat as many as you want. Are you sure you want to though? I wouldn't want you to spoil your precious diet."

A diet program never came up in their conversations. It didn't have to. Despite those pancakes at the diner—which could have been explained away by a cheat day or the fact that Mel didn't serve healthy food—Clark was the kind of man whose tight belts screamed, "I had exactly 1.1 ounces of cashew nuts today as a snack. That's exactly 143 calories and lots of good fats to fuel my crossfit workout later this afternoon." The tips of his ears went red and he reached for the cookies anyway, taking one into each hand. Kate followed his lead.

"It's a holiday, right? I can afford the calories."

"Then you admit it. A holiday *is* happening."

"Just because I don't celebrate it doesn't mean it's not happening. Besides..." They shared a meaningful look. What kind of meaning, Kate wasn't sure. But it meant something. Her insides churned. "I promised someone I'd give it the old college try."

On the surface, she liked the sound of that. He'd come down here not to fight with her or start another argument, but because he wanted to honor his promise to her. His absence until now stuck in her craw.

"Then why were you hiding?"

"I wasn't hiding," he retorted, mouth full of cookies.

"You carried me through a storm and then I didn't see you again. You were hiding."

They both chewed, savoring the subtle flavors of the fresh treats.

"I'm sorry about what happened."

"Why? I lived, didn't I?"

"Yeah, but—"

She flicked flour in his direction, failing to strike him with the white powder.

"I said I wanted an adventure, didn't I?" A big bite of cookie melted in her mouth. "Well, I got one."

"Listen." Clark clapped his hands together, ridding them of cookie dust and crumbs. "I promised someone I'd try this Christmas thing out, so what do I do?"

"Wanna help me make cookies?"

They didn't need anymore, but with three more trays of cookie dough and time to kill, Kate could think of no better option than this one.

"Is that a thing people do?" Clark raised an eyebrow; Kate almost choked.

"You're really out of the loop, there. Go into the other room and grab another one of these ornaments, will you?"

She raised the wire star she appropriated as a cookie-cutter. It glimmered in the low winter light. Clark left for the living room.

"You got it."

Kate dressed herself in a mothballed apron. In the next room, rustling and tinkling of ornamental bells danced in the air as Clark searched for a wire star. She continued their conversation through the door, raising her voice just enough to be heard.

"You're telling me you never made cookies around this time of year?"

A deep, masculine chuckle. "Are you fishing for my tragic backstory?"

"Only because I think you'll bite."

"You don't want to hear it."

He returned with the star in tow. Kate took her

place at the long kitchen island, which looked like a tiny winter wonderland. Flour covered the surface like perfect snowcapped mountains.

"You're admitting there is a tragic backstory."

"I didn't say that."

"You don't have to tell me." Mr. Woodward, Clark's uncle, was one of the kindest men Kate ever knew. As much as she liked to tease Clark about what he called his tragic backstory, she had a hard time believing she was opening up old wounds by asking after it. How could a man as good as Mr. Woodward allow someone as close to him as a nephew endure a miserable life? Kate assumed Clark had some kind of stigma associated with Christmas—maybe a girlfriend dumped him around the season or he was allergic to pine or something—but those were all easily solvable problems. If she could replace the sad memories with beautiful ones, maybe she could take away the lonely emptiness in his eyes. "I was thinking if I knew, maybe I could help."

Clark didn't speak right away. He went into a cabinet and found an apron of his own. As he pulled it over his head and rolled up the sleeves of his blue collared shirt, Kate stopped herself from breathing too loud. She'd thought he was handsome since she met him, but this was something else. The clash of the domestic apron with his strong, exposed forearms, his willingness to open up and be sensitive around her… Her cheeks flushed, and it had nothing to do with the blazing oven. When Clark returned, he spoke again.

"I haven't had a real Christmas since I was nine years old. If I ever did make cookies, it was so long ago it's impossible to remember if I did."

"Really?"

"Yeah." He clearly thought that would be the end of it. Holding up the star ornament, he stared at Kate through its negative space like a rich man assessing a stranger through a monocle. "Now, what do I do with this?"

On the marble countertops before them, Kate set up their station. A frozen pad of cookie dough waited on the floured countertop and a greased cookie sheet waited for the cut-out cookies. She demonstrated the method, every so often glancing at Clark to gauge his reaction.

"You just sprinkle some flour on it and press it in. Like so."

"I don't know." He hesitated over the preparations, suddenly skittish. "I don't want to ruin it."

"You can't ruin it. Just press in…" She demonstrated again, "And pull it out."

Clark breathed in deep, as though he were diffusing a bomb instead of cutting out cookies. It was a cute image, in a way. He'd been out of practice in having fun for so long, he couldn't even take something as simple as cutting out cookies any less seriously than negotiating a huge business deal. He laid the makeshift cookie-cutter into the dough, pulled it out, and fumbled to pick the newly made star up. There weren't many ways to mess up using a cookie-cutter, so Clark's clumsy attempt came out fairly neat. Two of the star's points were lopsided and inconsistent with the rest. Clark deflated.

"I messed up the ends. What do I do now?"

"Just put it on the tray and try again with another one," Kate said, obviously.

"But—"

"Not everything's a disaster, Clark. You can always try again."

"I can't—"

He stopped himself short, hesitating to finish his thought. Like a starving man given a bite of food only to have it taken away, Kate longed to hear it completed. What couldn't he do? And why couldn't he do it? She reminded herself to be grateful. For most of the day, he'd been as emotionally distant as he possibly could be. This was one of the first glimpses she got of his full emotional range. Even if his disappointment seemed silly to her, at least he was showing her some feeling. He could have kept himself closed off and private, deflecting her every attempt to get close to him. But he didn't. He was letting her see him for the first time. Kate stepped behind him, reaching her arms under his to better help him.

She didn't want to think about how good he smelled. Like an oaken whiskey barrel or a fresh forest. Nor did she want to think about how good his warmth felt mixing with hers. She didn't want to think about her desire to wrap her arms around his chest and hold him to her until he turned around and returned the gesture.

She didn't want to. But she did anyway.

"Let me help," she whispered, unable to catch her own stampeding breath.

Slowly, she guided his hands through the process, paying special attention to the tips of the stars.

"See?" She withdrew from him as he laid the star down on the cookie sheet, wanting to wipe the girlish swoon from her eyes before he could catch it. "Perfect."

"Thanks."

Was it her hope talking, or did he sound as breathless as she felt? Kate cleared her throat and returned to their task. Maybe talking about him would remove all of the magic tingles crossing her skin.

"Don't think you're getting out of it." She nudged him playfully with her shoulder. "Why haven't you had Christmas for twenty years?"

"I went to boarding school."

A diplomatic answer. Kate didn't accept it.

"And what? You never came back?"

"My parents died on New Year's. We'd just had our big family Christmas. I was only nine." Her lungs stopped working as he delivered his story with matter-of-fact sincerity. Her hands stilled over the cookies, but Clark went on cutting. "They were up in Eagle Point. I was here with my uncle. They went to a party and never came home. They told me a drunk driver lost control on a patch of black ice."

"Oh, Clark. I didn't mean... I'm so sorry. I didn't know."

Such a small way to apologize for something so massive, but Kate couldn't think of anything else to say. The gears of comprehension ground together in her head as information flew at her. She pieced it together. It all led to one heartbreaking picture.

"That's why I was so afraid of the forest. When they told me, I just ran out there. I didn't bring a flashlight or anything. I just ran through the rain until I couldn't see the house anymore. My uncle came out and found me eventually, but I was..." He rubbed a rough hand over his face. "He took custody of me, but I begged to go to boarding school. I didn't want to be here and remember. I didn't want The Christmas Company reminding me of what happened. That's part of the reason I hate it so much. I didn't want to think of Christmas ever again. So, I stayed at school almost all year round."

He shook his head. "On the one hand, it made me the man I am today. I pinch pennies because I'm afraid if I spend a cent out of line I'll lose the company. The only thing of them I still have. I wear my father's old suit jackets because I don't want to lose them. I stayed in school and worked all the time to make them proud, to become the great man they would have wanted me to be. On the other hand...staying at school made it easier to avoid thinking about it. No matter how much my uncle begged me to come home even for a weekend, I just couldn't face being here. I wanted to hold onto them, but I didn't want to remember them, either. It was too painful. Now, it's like I pushed it all away for so long, I can barely remember even when I want to."

"Why?"

"What do you mean, *why*?"

"I mean...why are you telling me all this? You could have just lied."

All at once, she became aware of tears blurring her vision as she gazed up at him. Tears for a man who'd lost everything. He'd been defeated by the world again and again, all while she'd been basking in the attention he'd been denied. The cookie-cutter remained useless in her limp hand. Clark sighed and put his own down to turn and meet her.

"Because this is the first Christmas no one let me be alone. The first time I pushed everyone away but..." They shared a meaningful look, one filled with the warmth of a freshly lit fireplace. "Someone stayed anyway."

She wanted to hold him. Or kiss him. Anything to show him he didn't deserve to be alone. Keeping her hands and lips to herself, she swiftly changed the subject, breaking the emotionally devastating mood with one joking question.

"How am I doing so far on that front? Have I made an elf of you?"

"You know, it's not so bad. I don't see what the fuss is all about yet, but I'm warming up to it. Keep feeding me these cookies and maybe I'll like it even more."

In a few swift movements, he placed the full baking sheet into the oven and plucked a few cookies off of the cooling rack.

"The good news is that we'll have enough cookies to last us three lifetimes."

"You don't know how many cookies I can eat."

He handed her a stack of five cookies, and Kate's stomach both curdled and leapt for joy. The idea of so many cookies was appealing, but the reality frightened her stomach. She almost refused the gift. Then, the smell hit her. She was powerless to the combination of sugar and butter cooked to warm perfection.

"If I eat more than twenty, drop a piano on my head," she encouraged, accepting the stack. "It's the only way to stop me once I get into a feeding frenzy."

"Deal." He laughed, a sound sweeter than any cookies.

They snacked in silence. Though this huge revelation hung between them, things seemed less fraught between them. Still, Kate couldn't help but sink in the sadness she'd heard in his voice. Cookies weren't enough to erase that memory.

"Hey, Clark?" she asked.

"Yeah?"

"What do you remember about Christmas? You said you don't remember much. Do you remember anything?"

Clark hesitated, then shook his head. "I haven't thought about it in so long."

"Do you want to remember? You don't have to. I know it's hard," she assured him.

Kate thought of her parents every day. She couldn't imagine the pain of wanting to forget them, of hiding away at boarding school so no one could make you think of them.

"I remember..." Clark bit his bottom lip. His hands flexed. He leaned against the counter for support. A tiny, tiny smile glowed on his softened face. "My mother's perfume. Tuberose, I think. I remember them dragging me to go caroling. Every year, my mom would make a tub of hot cocoa and my dad would help her make cookies and we'd walk through the neighborhood caroling. None of us could sing, really. Dad was the worst of us, but it didn't matter. It was fun." He lost himself in the thoughts of his past. "When my mom would tuck me in on Christmas Eve, I remember she'd light a candle and put it on my windowsill. She told me it was so Santa knew where to find me."

"Those are beautiful memories."

"I miss them. I haven't let myself think about them like this in so long, but...I miss them." He trailed off, staring out into the distance. But no sooner had he withdrawn than he brought himself back, clearing his throat as if to clear the air of his very self. "Sorry. You don't want to hear this."

"I don't mind at all. In fact, it's pretty nice."

"Cookies and sad stories. What next? Champagne and a dentist appointment?" He chuckled, but the light didn't quite meet his eyes. Kate wanted nothing more than to sit here and talk to him about this forever. She wanted to know everything about him. What was his favorite shade of blue? What had his life been like after boarding school? What did he dream about?

For now, the questions would have to wait. As much as she wanted to keep talking, he needed something else. He needed a distraction. He still needed to fall in love with Christmas.

"Well." She smiled, her fingers brushing the top of his hand reassuringly. "The tree still isn't decorated."

New memories would never replace a lifetime of horrible ones, but Kate could at least give him one special night.

Chapter Twelve

I can't believe I told her. I can't believe I told her.
For the entire thirteen-step journey from the kitchen into the Christmas tree-dominated living room, Clark could only repeat those words. Then the thought mutated. *I can't believe I'm happy I told her. I can't believe I'm relieved I told her. I can't believe I trusted her. And still trust her.*

Clark couldn't remember the last time he'd thought about his parents for any stretch of time, much less talked about them. He treated his memory of them like a precious, finite resource. The more he shared them, the less he had for himself. If he talked about them too much, he feared, he'd lose them forever. He wanted to protect the pieces of them he could.

But talking about them with Kate liberated him. Secrets he'd been jealously hiding all his life came to the surface, excavating the pieces of his heart he'd buried long ago.

Before his parents died, they spent most of their

winter holidays here, visiting for a few days between Christmas and New Year's, reveling in the time they got to spend with their family. The living room hadn't changed. At least, it hadn't physically changed since Clark saw it last. No one came in and threw extra tinsel on the mantel or hung more fake icicles from the ceiling. But as night cloaked the Woodward House, the quality of light changed inside the opulent family room. Instead of another room in a house on a cold winter's day, it grew into a safe harbor of golden light, a refuge from the black night settling in outside of the walls. Kate turned the key in the fireplace, igniting the flames within and adding to the invisible layer of coziness wrapping itself around Clark's shoulders. It reminded him of the time *before*, of the winter evenings spent here with his aunt and uncle, his mother and father.

"I'm guessing you haven't decorated a tree in a while, either?"

"I did a couple of times at school. That sort of celebration was mandatory."

As a kid, Clark did everything to get out of the festivities required of boarding school boys to make them feel more at home during the season. Thinking about Christmas brought up those memories he fought so hard to hide and hold onto; participating in the jolly holiday with his schoolmates only made things worse. He feigned illnesses. He tried to get in-school suspension. He claimed religious exemption, even going as far as to wear a yarmulke for three months. All to no avail. The administration allowed him to remain on campus for the holidays, but refused to excuse him from celebrating that same holiday during term time.

"I guess you made handprint wreaths and stuff," Kate ventured as she dragged a stack of boxes out into the middle of the room. Clark raced to help her, taking the top three boxes away to lighten her load. He followed her lead, opening the tops and exposing the blinding treasure trove of glitter, red paint, and homey paper stars tucked inside.

"We mostly made pinecone reindeer. Our teachers were not the most imaginative bunch."

"That's a shame. The teachers here in Miller's Point are amazing." Kate picked out a chain of paperclip stars. Their lopsided shapes assured him they were the handiwork of school children. He wondered if any of them hated Christmas as much as he had when he was a boy. Did anyone in Miller's Point hate the season, or was he the only Grinch in sight? "Help me untangle these?"

"Yeah, sure."

With delicate fingers, they picked apart the tangled knots of nickel. Clark paid special attention not to bend them out of shape. Frivolous as he thought the exercise was for a classroom—when he was a boy, he threatened to file suit because Christmas activities robbed him of the teaching time his family paid for—someone still spent their time and effort on this chain of stars. He didn't want to ruin them. As they worked,

Kate talked, stupefying him more and more with every word out of her mouth.

"Miss Monzalno, the second-grade teacher, she teaches her kids how to make advent calendars. And Miss White takes her kids to Dallas every year to serve at a soup kitchen right before they get out for Christmas. I don't know if she still does it, but when I was there, Miss Elias took all of us to plant our own trees."

"You know so much about this town," he said, causing her to balk. A swift tug of her wrist sent the paperclip strand flying out of his hands.

She deflected. "It's mine. It's special to me."

"Not even Michael knew so much as you do."

"Miller's Point is my family."

"I don't know that much about *my* family."

He didn't mean it as an accusation. But she took it as one.

"You're not the only one with a tragic backstory, Clark."

"You...?" She faced the world with the blinding optimism of someone who'd never been hurt before. He'd assumed she had a brimming family with many siblings. Every time he so much as imagined her home life, he pictured a Norman Rockwell painting, a white picket fenced house with a table of smiling cousins and grandparents.

She made herself busy with the ornaments, taking them out one at a time and arranging them on the tree's branches. They sparkled ironically as a shadow took hold of Kate.

"My mom wasn't ever really in the picture and my dad was...not a good father." Those words hung in the air for a moment before she amended herself. What came next was a confession, one he wondered if she'd ever shared with another person so explicitly. "He was an alcoholic. I started volunteering with The Christmas Company when my teacher—Miss Sanders—wanted to help get me out of the house. I liked it so much, I never wanted to go back home. The town became more of my family than my family ever was. Not exactly tragic. It's really a happy ending, if you think about it."

Each word was worse than a kick in the teeth. It took Clark a long, solemn moment before he recovered enough to speak again.

"Only you could see it that way."

"See it what way?"

"Horrible people treated you horribly and you think it's a blessing?" he asked, furrowing his brow. Kate only shrugged, picking up a small, golden star and hanging it up on a branch. The rustle of needles filled Clark's nose with the scent of pine, a scent he'd forever associate with this moment and this confounding, exceptional woman.

Her shoulders were so slender for someone who carried the weight of the world on them without so much as bowing beneath the pressure.

"If I was a normal person with a normal life, I

never would have found anything spectacular. You know, bad things aren't the end of the story. Well, I guess they can be, but only if you let them."

A million incredulous, confused responses bubbled to Clark's lips. He didn't speak any of them. She offered him simplicity. What was the point in complicating something that clearly guided her and gave her happiness? Changing the subject before he could contemplate whether he could have lived his life like she lived hers, Clark reached for the nearest box of ornaments. He cleared his throat.

"How do you decorate this thing? And where did all of these come from?"

"It's all Christmas Company stock," she explained, "but we have this tradition where every year everyone who works for the festival brings one ornament and adds it to the collection. That's why they don't match."

"And what's the point of that?"

"I don't know. It's just fun."

"But why?"

"Because it's a tradition."

"But why is it a tradition? How did it start? What's the big deal?" Clark honestly wasn't trying to be an annoying jerk. He simply didn't get it, like his twelve-year-old self didn't get the point of the Christmas traditions at boarding school. Everyone bought into the rituals and empty gestures; he didn't understand why.

"It just is." Kate's hands hesitated over a small puppy ornament, searching for something to offer him. Clark held his breath. "Like your mom putting out the Santa candle. It didn't actually do anything. It's just meaningful for its own sake."

"Wait...you mean Santa isn't real?"

He chose to joke rather than acknowledge his own investment in his mother's tradition. That was different. It earned him a good-natured shove from his partner.

"Of course he's real. Shut up and decorate the tree."

Obediently, Clark collected a few ornaments out of the box, inspecting each one with keen interest. They didn't come out of a two-for-one sale from some big box store. Each one came from a person here in town. Each one carried meaning. They were, like the paperclip stars, special to someone. Maybe if he knew why, everything would become clear.

"Can you tell me about them?" he asked.

"The ornaments?"

"Yeah. Do you know anything about them?"

"I know them all. I keep the record books about who gives us what." She collected a few herself. "Why don't you start putting them up and I'll talk you through them?"

Clark nodded, then reached up on his toes to place a toy X-wing fighter up towards the top of the tree.

"What's the deal with this one?"

"It's heavy!" Kate held out a hand to stop him, her fingers barely brushing his. Panic gleamed in her eyes. Clark reminded himself how important these little trinkets were to her. Breaking even one would break a piece of her. "Put it on a low branch. The high branches aren't strong enough to hold it."

"Right."

Great move, Clark. Now she thinks you're a triple moron. You don't get Christmas and you made her confess her life story to you and *you don't get basic physics.* He placed the miniature space plane on the appropriate branch, ignoring the heat rising to the tops of his ears. If she noticed the red splotches undoubtedly forming there, she was decent enough not to mention anything.

"Teddy Cooper gave us that two years ago. He got it in a happy meal, said it was the "happiest meal of his life," and so he turned it into an ornament so he could always remember."

"Wow. Okay..." Clark scraped his memory for the last time he'd laughed as much as he laughed today, only to come up empty. Brushing that thought away, he picked up a tiny gold band turned into an ornament by an interlocked strand of clear fishing line. He dangled it so close to his eyes his lashes brushed the circlet of metal, trying to discern what it could possibly be. "What about this one?"

"Condola Walker. She broke off her engagement and that's the ring."

"What?" The urge to throw the ring across the room fought his urge to run into town and return the jewelry to this Condola person. Who would give up something so expensive when they could have just pawned it? Kate, unmoved by his indignation, rolled her eyes.

"It was, like, twelve dollars or something. Believe me, she was glad to be rid of it. Keep 'em coming. We'll never get this tree decorated at this rate."

Shaking off the abject strangeness of someone just giving away their engagement ring, Clark hung it up towards the top of the tree. It caught the light, spinning in the gentle breeze of the drafty old house. Even if he wasn't inclined to like her—which he was, he'd admitted defeat in his battle against his affection for Kate—he'd still be the first to admit how impressive Kate's instant recall of the facts of the town was. Like a close-hand magic trick, Clark all at once wanted to move in closer and step further back. Her confession about her childhood rattled him; the distraction of decorating didn't prove as distancing as he hoped. She'd been so broken by her family that she'd devoted her life to everyone else in this town.

No wonder they all came at her call today. No wonder they decorated his house and cooked a banquet at her request.

"This one's a tiny fake tree," Clark said, twirling the small carving. Kate wedged herself between the wall and the tree, trying to decorate an unseen portion of branches, so this one demanded some description.

"Does it have little red baubles on it?" she asked, muffled by the tree between them.

"Yes."

"That one's from Mr. and Mrs. Simon. Their little grandbaby died, and Mrs. Simon built the coffin herself out of a tree in their backyard. She took a piece of the scrap wood and carved that."

Clark cradled the tiny ornament in the palm of his hands, staring down at it reverently as he searched for a word to properly describe the empty cavern opening in his chest. He hadn't felt this way in so long.

"That's sad."

"Don't worry. There are plenty of funny ones in there." Kate came to the rescue as Clark placed the tiny tree in a high place of honor upon the larger tree. "Do you see any paper flowers made out of thick paper? They should have music notes on them, if that helps."

Digging around, he finally found not one, but about twenty of those flowers tucked into a shoebox in the bottom of one of the ornament crates.

"Yeah."

"Those were given to us by Pastor Mark, but he didn't make them. He caught a bunch of boys making paper airplanes out of hymnal pages, so he decided if they liked folding paper so much, they would take all two hundred of the out-of-date hymnals and make paper flowers out of them. They spent six days of Christmas vacation making those things."

They carried on in this fashion for longer than Clark cared to admit; even worse, he hung on her every word. He actually invested himself in the intersecting and interweaving lives of these strangers. A born storyteller, Kate shared every story she remembered, dragging him deeper and deeper into the melting-pot mythologies of Miller's Point.

His attention slipped only once, when he pulled out what seemed like the millionth star-shaped trinket. Only, this one was different. It struck him. Multiple shades of ugly green and brown glass had been melted together to form a sort of patchwork glass star. Its edges created an outline out of twisted wire. The most similar thing he could think of was a stained-glass window, but those were beautiful. This wasn't quite beautiful. It was sublime, perhaps. Holding it up to the light, he let the color play on his face, losing himself in the warped surface of the star.

"What's this one?"

"That's one of mine," Kate said, her voice dipping low. The pride she'd taken only a few minutes ago in her stories and shared histories vanished.

"What is it? Did you make it?" Clark squinted, coming up closer to a raised etching along one of the corners. He could hardly make it out. "Is this a whiskey label? I didn't know you drank."

"I don't."

"Was this like an art project or something?"

After hours of learning about her town and these ornaments, he should have known none of these were *just* anything. They all carried their own weighted tales. To think Kate's wouldn't was the height of foolishness.

"When my dad died, right after my eighteenth birthday, I went to his apartment and cleaned it all out. I hadn't been living there for, like, two years. Emily's family took me in. So, I went through the whole house, throwing almost everything away. And then I got to my old bedroom. It was covered in broken bottles, like he'd just thrown them all at the wall and let them shatter. There had to be a hundred of them. He used my room as a garbage can, basically." She laughed a wry laugh.

It occurred to Clark then how unfamiliar they were, and yet how close at the same time. They'd only met yesterday, but they'd both exchanged their most painful memories without a second thought. Maybe it was the magic of the season or her persistence or a little bit of both, but they trusted one another even when they had every reason to protect their own secrets.

He'd broken her once. He told her he didn't care. He lied. But this moment was different. She wasn't broken; she wasn't hiding. But he still wanted to wrap her in his arms and hold her together.

"Kate—"

"Anyway," she brushed him off. "I cleaned the whole house, but I couldn't get rid of all that glass. I mean, I could have. But when the whole house was clean and I was left with a handful of broken glass shards, I didn't want to. I wanted something of his, even if he hated me. I asked Michael to help me make this. My dad wasn't a good dad. Or really a dad at all. But he was mine. And I didn't want him to be erased. I wanted to always look at the tree and remember."

"Remember what?"

Her arms froze over the tree. The whiskey bottle star halted over the greenery. Her face knitted tightly in an expression he'd never seen come across her face before.

"I don't know," she confessed. "Remember him. Remember that I survived. Remember that I forgave him and loved him even if he wasn't good to me."

"You forgave him?"

Kate blinked. Her long eyelashes were wet with tears, but none fell down her cheeks. Her stare melted into confusion, as if he was a student who'd just asked what the capital of their own state was, as if the answer was so obvious as to render the question absurd.

"I had to."

"Why?" He asked.

Somehow, Clark and Kate had gotten so close he could feel her breath on his skin. He wanted to kiss the wrinkle between her eyebrow away. He wanted to hold her and tell her nothing could ever hurt her again.

"Because we can't survive if we're always carrying dead bodies around, you know? That's no way to make a happy life." The sting of conviction stole the breath from Clark's lungs. He was guilty. He'd been dragging around dead bodies his entire life, robbing himself of any chance of happiness just so he could forget his own pain. Kate rolled her eyes, an attempt to clear the air of tension. "Besides, he was kind of a jerk. He probably would have resented my forgiveness. No better way to get revenge, right?"

She moved to step away, but Clark caught her. He couldn't help but touch her. Their intimacy demanded it. His cold hand reached up for her left cheek; he cradled it, commanding her eyes. Her breath hitched. His heart stumbled. *Kiss her, you moron* argued with *don't ruin what you have by kissing her, you moron.* He'd gone most of his life without friends, and tonight he'd found one. Learning from her and basking in their friendship had to be more important than kissing her.

"How do you do it?"

"Do what?"

"Stay as hopeful as you do. I don't understand how it's possible for one person to be this optimistic all the time. I was awful to you and you didn't flinch. Your life hasn't been great but you count it as a blessing… How do you do it?"

"You really want to know?"

"Yeah."

She bit her lip, an adorable gesture Clark never got in movies but now understood completely. She grew increasingly sheepish as she interrogated his motives.

"You promise you won't make fun of me? It's pretty cheesy."

"Promise."

"Cross your heart?"

"Yeah."

She shot him a look. Apparently, she wanted him to *actually* cross his heart. He did so, all while struggling to maintain a dignified, solemn expression. When she was satisfied, she shoved her hands into her back pockets, staring up at the tree. In the glow of the lights, she looked more than beautiful as she whispered the simple truth that had sustained her through her entire life.

"I keep Christmas with me all year long. It's the one time of year when I find it impossible to think the worst in people. If I pretend every day is Christmas, it makes life so much easier to live. And people so much easier to love."

"I wish I could do that," Clark breathed. He tried to move his hand away from her cheek, but Kate got there first. She held him there, this time forcing him to give her his eyes. A sweet smile encouraged him. Challenged him. Filled him with hope.

"You can."

Chapter Thirteen

Tree decorating gave way to black-and-white movies and popcorn, which gave way to leftover turkey sandwiches with cranberry sauce which inevitably gave way to heavy eyelids and almost naps. Conversation and laughter flowed easily between them, though Kate got the distinct feeling Clark was out of practice when it came to having a friend. The defenses he threw up against her only this morning diffused, leaving them only with his rusty attempts at humor and near-constant questions about Christmas and its traditions. Kate didn't mind at all. In fact, she suspected this Christmas would go down as one of her favorites. Not because it was perfect—it definitely wasn't—but because she'd never experienced anything quite like this, something this pure.

The Festival was her life. Everyone who worked on it was her family. She was immeasurably glad for the security they gave her. The problem came on Christmas night, when her entire year had been leading up to a grand spectacle of the season. She loved the spectacle, but there was something beautiful and singular about sharing a private Christmas with someone who'd never had one before. For the first time, Kate saw the holiday not through her eyes, but his. The beauty of this holiday she loved so much now engulfed her. The lights shone brighter. The classic lines of *It's a Wonderful Life* cut deeper. Her faith renewed.

When *It's a Wonderful Life* went into its encore showing, Kate stretched her tight muscles along the overstuffed couch. Clark, for his part, sprawled out in a distinctly Victorian armchair. Wide, decorative walls of the chair obscured his face behind their panels while the roaring fireplace illuminated his long limbs.

"Clark? Clark, are you awake?" she whispered. Half of her didn't want to disturb him, while the other half of her demanded she wake him up. It wasn't even midnight, after all. There was so much Christmas left and so little time to prove its worth to him. Fortunately, he saved her the trouble of waking him.

"Yeah, I'm awake," he whispered back, as though they were in a crowded movie theater instead of his own living room.

The next phase of Kate's plan wasn't really for him. It wasn't even part of the plan. She'd been doing Christmas without parents for most of her life, which meant she was fairly stuck in her ways. There was one tradition she refused to compromise on.

"I was wondering... Do you have a copy of *A Christmas Carol*?"

"No idea. Why?"

"I read it every Christmas Eve."

She thought she'd brought her own copy for such a scenario, but a quick scan of her backpack earlier in the evening revealed only pajamas, a change of clothes for Christmas Day, a toothbrush, and a box of white chocolate pretzels. Perhaps during her packing she assumed the multimillion-dollar mansion would contain at least one copy of the greatest novella in the English canon; if she had a manor and an estate, she'd have a million copies. It was, after all, her favorite book.

"Really? But don't you..." Clark leaned forward, popping out from behind the panels of his chair to scoff in disbelief, "You basically watch *A Christmas Carol* every day for like, a month and a half, don't you?"

"Yeah, but..." Kate played with her hands. One of the reasons she'd gotten the job at the festival was her reputation in town as the "Dickens-obsessed girl." She could practically recite the original book by heart. What they didn't know was that after the festival ended on Christmas night, she tucked herself into her bed at her dad's house and read the book over and over again, just so she could pretend she was still in a magical world of hope and joy, rather than a booze-soaked nightmare. Kate didn't feel inclined to tell Clark the entire truth, so she danced around it instead. "Usually, once the festival is over, I go home and I'm too keyed up to sleep. It's my favorite book, so it puts me in a good mood."

"Follow me," Clark said, rising to his feet.

"Where are we going?"

"If it's anywhere, it'll be in the library. C'mon."

Kate caught a passing glimpse of the library earlier, but walking in and fully immersing herself in it almost knocked her back a step. She'd never been in this room before. It was off-limits during all Christmas Company events. Belle's library in *Beauty and The Beast* had nothing on this beautiful collection of leather-bound tomes. The Woodward Library in the center of town, until now Kate's favorite place in the world, paled in comparison. She thought back to the stack of three rotating library books on her bedside table and her falling-apart copy of *A Christmas Carol*. Rich people may not have had it easy, as Clark's stories about his childhood suggested, but they *did* have an endless supply of books, which Kate could absolutely get on board with.

"There must be a million books in here," Kate said, awed.

"I think it's closer to two thousand. Let's check the card catalogue."

"There's a card catalogue?"

"How else would you find anything?" Clark arrived at a carved wooden chest pockmarked with orderly drawers. Each was labeled with a series of letters. He rifled through the *Da-Dl* drawer, moving the cards with practiced efficiency. Kate could only assume he was too cheap to digitize his office. Everything in Woodward Enterprises probably operated on card catalogue. "Dickens... Dickens... *Oliver Twist. Tale of Two Cities, A... Pickwick Papers...* I'm sorry. No *A Christmas Carol.*"

To his credit, Clark really did sound sorry. This morning, he probably would have jumped for joy and rubbed the absence of the classic story in her face. The taste in Kate's mouth bittered with disappointment.

"Maybe it's somewhere else?"

"No, I don't think so," Clark said, even as he dug through the catalogue for a missing or misplaced card. "But why don't you read it off your phone?"

"That's not the same."

She realized how petulant and selfish the refusal made her sound; she didn't care.

"It's a shame. I've never read it."

They'd discussed this character flaw of his before, but now Kate felt she could really shine. All her life prepared her for this moment. Adopting a practiced British accent, she dipped into the same performative storytelling style she often did when reading the abridged children's version to the little ones in the festival cast.

"*Marley was dead: to begin with. There is no doubt whatever about that. The register of his burial was signed by the clerk...*" Kate stopped. That wasn't right. "No. *Was signed by the clergyman, the undertaker...*" Again, she messed up. "No..."

When she looked back up, Clark graciously hid his laughter behind a hand clenched over his mouth.

"Are you trying to recite it right now?" He managed between tightly gritted teeth.

"I used to have it basically memorized."

"Is that a brag?"

"It's a tradition," she defended as they made their way through the illuminated house back to the pine-scented living room.

"Then read it on your phone."

"You don't get it. The book itself is important. It takes me to Victorian England. Reading it on my phone reminds me I'm here in this time and this place. The paper is a medium across time."

"Listen. I like you, but you are a huge nerd. You know that, right?"

Despite her disappointment, Kate laughed. It wasn't the first time she'd heard that and it wouldn't be the last, but coming from Clark who cobbled his own shoes and whispered when the TV was on, it was a hilarious accusation to hear. "No one knows better than me."

But if loving Christmas and trying to get others to love it too made her a nerd, then she gladly accepted the title, and nothing could ever make her give it up. Especially now, when Clark looked at her the way he did, like she had all the answers to his questions about finding joy in this world.

Her mission for a copy of *A Christmas Carol* thoroughly defeated, they returned to the living room, though for what, Kate couldn't quite decide. Going to bed now would be akin to admitting defeat. She still wasn't convinced he cared enough about this day or this town or the festival. And, if she was being honest with herself, she didn't want to leave him. He was, against all her better judgment, fun to be around. She was enjoying herself, even without the trappings of her usual traditions.

Emily, no doubt, would have accused her of seeing him with rose-tinted glasses. Emily *always* said Kate's willingness to like people without any proof of their goodness was a sign of her naivete. Maybe she was right. Kate saw it a different way. She didn't need proof of someone's goodness. Their being a person made them good; she just had to find where that good was buried. Today, Clark's humanity peeked out through her excavation of his heart.

On second thought, maybe it was better to think about him like a butterfly stabbed on a cork board. If she thought about him that way, she'd stop thinking about wanting to kiss him or hold his broken pieces back together.

As they navigated the maze of hallways and doors between the library and the living room—Kate finally understood how the game *Clue* came about; if the house in that game and movie was anything like this house, in that game and movie was anything like this house, it's a wonder they ever found the body at all— Kate whistled absently to herself, a habit she'd had since she was a kid. It got her in trouble with teachers, her father, and coworkers, so when she realized she was doing it now, she braced herself for the worst. Clark didn't like music, especially Christmas music. The worst never came; the whistling only stopped when they walked into the living room to the sound of the mantel-place clock tolling the hour. It matched her heartbeat, vibrating at the same frequency. *Bom... Bom... Midnight. Bom... Bom... Midnight. Bom... Bom... Midnight.* Unlike Cinderella, Kate's magic remained when the clock stilled, and the prince didn't disappear.

Not that she saw Clark as a prince. Definitely not. Of course not.

"What now? What do we do now?" Clark asked, a jagged edge serrating his enthusiastic voice. Did he... Did he think they were going to kiss? Like on New Year's Eve? Quick thinking would be needed to avoid any confusion. A list of random activities ran out of her, activities she could use to wedge herself even closer to him without actually getting *close* to him. In this scenario she'd gotten herself into, Kate existed in the middle of a seesaw. Tipping too far to one side would keep her from her task, from saving her town. Tipping too far to the other would leave her vulnerable to Clark's half-smiles and thawing eyes.

"There's plenty we can do." She paced. "Sometimes people toast marshmallows. Or get out a telescope and look out for Santa. We could call NORAD."

"What do *you* usually do at this time on Christmas Eve? You're the expert. Let's do what you do."

Rats. She was hoping he wouldn't ask that. The midnight tolls on the big clock in the center of Miller's Point always meant one thing, and one thing only on December 24: the midnight ball. On a night when the festival *wasn't* cancelled by a profit-hungry but secretly beautiful-souled out-of-towner, every volunteer and staff member would get dressed in their 1843 best and go straight to the town square, where the guests would be invited to join them for a traditional Victorian ball, complete with warm mulled wine, a live string band, and a fake snowdrift. As the last official event of the night, the twirling and dipping and bowing and swirling lasted well into the early hours of the morning. It wasn't unusual for the younger members, Kate included, to dance until their shoes broke and the sun rose over the tops of the buildings. Then, they'd welcome Christmas morning with hot chocolate and leftovers from the previous day's feast before preparing themselves for the Christmas Day crowds.

But dancing would mean getting close to Clark physically...and that would mean the possibility of getting too close to him emotionally. She'd read and believed in enough Jane Austen books to know it only took one dance to fall in love with someone. One minute you're dancing, the next everything else in the world disappears but the one person you're meant to be with.

If she danced with him, she could lose her heart to him.

...It also occurred to her she might have been overreacting about the entire thing.

It just wasn't a chance she was willing to take.

"I don't think it's really your kind of thing," she brushed him off, searching the room for something else to do. Popcorn garlands? Gingerbread houses?

"None of this is my thing. I hate all of this. But I'm trying it for you."

"Why?"

"Because I promised I would."

"You still don't like it?"

"I still don't like it." His hands flexed. "But I don't hate it either."

Worse people hurled worse things at Kate on a regular basis. Out-of-towners coming in for the festival called her crazy, a zealot for Christmas. They tacked horrible names to her when she pulled them out of the crowd after overindulging on mulled wine or when she confiscated their flasks from their bags. Yet, Clark's tacit admission sliced her in half. She was failing. He still didn't believe.

Fine. If he wanted it that way, if he wanted to throw her through the motions without ever really opening himself up to genuine change, fine. She could play his game. Her hands gripped the material of her jeans at the hips.

"We dance. There's this big dance in the center of town. Everyone goes."

"I don't dance," Clark said, just as she knew he would. Almost every activity she proposed received some sort of push back from him; she expected nothing less from this challenge. If he didn't cut loose enough to know how to decorate a Christmas tree, of course he wouldn't dance. Dance required an openness of the heart she wasn't convinced he actually possessed.

"No?" she pressed, biting in her own confidence even as he sunk into the nearest chair and seemed content to stay there forever, if possible.

"No."

As Clark sank into the armchair, he wondered vaguely if he could literally melt into the fabric and disappear. When that line of thought proved frivolous, he made himself a promise: *You will not get up and dance with her. No matter how much she might want you to. Don't you dare do it. You've made a fool of yourself a hundred times over today, but draw the line here. Dancing is a stupid, pointless activity and you're not—I repeat, not—going to do it. Especially not with Kate.*

His place in the corner of the room afforded Clark the perfect view of Kate's preparations. Bickering words popped between them like whacked baseballs as she dragged furniture towards the walls. A few hours ago, a move like that would have earned her Clark's annoyance, annoyance he now knew to be fruitless. She'd gotten her way all day. Objecting earned him no points with her.

This time, though, she wouldn't get her way.

Let her turn the room into a pseudo-ballroom if she wanted. He wouldn't join her.

"Why don't you dance?" she asked. The smug smile tugging her pink lips told Clark everything he needed to know. She thought she was going to get her way with enough prodding. Well, the joke was on her. He was in his chair and in his chair he would stay.

"I just don't."

"You don't do Christmas either," Kate reminded him.

"I'm putting my foot down at prancing around the room like a drunken reindeer."

"Someone's grumpy."

"There's no way you're getting me to dance."

The coda of that sentence, *with you*, never made it out of his mouth. In his mind, there was a distinct difference between not wanting to dance at all and not wanting to dance with her specifically.

Floor clear, Kate pulled off the little slip-on red and green shoes she'd been wearing with her pajamas, leaving her feet covered by an equally busy pair of socks covered in a pattern of Santa sleighs.

"I didn't want to dance with you anyway. I can dance on my own."

"Good. Enjoy yourself."

He reached for a nearby newspaper. The headline read something about the end of The Christmas Company. That page ended up discarded on the floor; the comics section always interested him more than any part of a newspaper, anyway. Determined to ignore Kate and whatever stunt she pulled, Clark only glanced up in time to see Kate walk over to the couch and coquettishly solicit an imaginary suitor for a dance.

"Me? You want to dance with me?"

"Really?" Clark deadpanned.

"I'd be delighted," she told the imaginary man as she took his invisible hand and led him to the newly made dance floor. Without a triumphant smirk in his direction, her lips wrapped around the whistling notes of a Christmas tune Clark heard a million times before but couldn't quite place off the top of his head.

"You're making a fool of yourself."

"I think you're making a fool out of yourself. You're letting a beautiful woman dance alone."

Beautiful woman. She was that and so much more. Clever. Decisive. Loving. Damaged and beyond hopeful. Over the top of his newspaper, he watched her, this woman who invaded his house, his life and perhaps his heart. Watching her directly would make her think she'd won. Discretion was key here.

Clark lived firmly in the real world. Two feet on the ground. Head firmly out of the clouds. Business. Practicality. Frugality. These ideals guided his simple, prosperous and quiet life. He didn't like superhero franchises or any books about unrealistically clever detectives. Movies rarely made an appearance on his weekly leisure schedule. Television, even less frequently. He saw the world and everyone in it as they were, not as how they wanted to be seen or as he wanted to see them.

...Then Kate curtseyed to an imaginary partner, and Clark's firm grip on reality dissolved in a haze of magic, magic he didn't believe in or trust, but that took hold of him all the same.

Before his eyes, the world changed, as easily as turning a page in a book. Kate no longer stood in socked feet on an ancient rug. Her partner wasn't invisible. Her pajamas were replaced with a ball gown. Her hair swept up into an elaborate updo. The living room was a ballroom, decorated even more grandly for Christmas than before. An orchestra replaced her whistling. A handsome man lifted her and swanned her around the room, making her fall more and more in love with him every step they took together.

And Clark was jealous. Jealous of an apparition. His throat dried. His chest tightened. Leaving her to dance with this imagined rival was no longer possible.

He stepped into this new reality, this historical fairy tale he conjured around them. He crossed the ballroom. His heart pounded louder than the orchestra. And he tapped the stranger on his black suit-clad shoulder.

"May I cut in?"

When Kate's face sparked into an all-consuming smile, his heart rate quieted and the music once again dominated the room.

"I'd be delighted."

The language was as dated as the fantasy, but she

was very much real, a fact only confirmed when her warm hand found its way into his while the other placed itself on his shoulder. His found her waist. They drew close. Close enough to fall in love.

"I don't know how to dance like this," he confessed.

"Just follow my lead."

Kate stepped simply, nudging him along. Never judging his lack of confidence or shouting out when his foot accidentally grazed her toes. Soon, he got the hang of it, and they flew across the floor like dolls in a music box. His heart grew. And grew. And grew. Until he thought it would explode right out of his chest and hand itself over to her forever.

In this dance, he saw everything he'd been denying himself his entire life: the chance to be free. Not only of his past, but of his own fears and hatred of the world. By trying to protect himself, he'd robbed himself of simple, easy joys like dancing.

And falling in love.

Not that he would have fallen in love before this moment. There was no one on earth like Kate Buckner, and even if he'd been looking for love before now, he wouldn't have found it. It existed in her and her alone. And now, he'd found it.

As they twirled and tripped and floated across the floor, Kate whistled the tune, her eyes never leaving his face and his never leaving hers. Could she feel his heartbeat? Could she hear it? Could she make out the Morse code of its beating? *Bum... Bum... I think I... Bum... Bum... Love you.*

They spun out and stopped their movements when Kate's song wound to a close. Unmoving, they held one another as if they hadn't stopped the waltz. Her eyes seemed to be made for him to admire. The perfect color. The perfect shape. The perfect windows into a perfect soul.

Was he crazy enough to think she felt this way too?

"I have some bad news," Kate whispered, too close to him to speak at a normal volume. Clark's hands shook.

"What's that?"

A glance upward. A guilty smile.

"We're under the mistletoe."

Sure enough. Green leaves and white berries dangled overhead.

"You know the tradition, don't you?" she asked.

Nodding, not trusting himself to speak, he waited for her to answer the unspoken questions hovering in the air between them. There was no way she didn't hear his heart now.

"Would you..." The whisper trailed off. Clark moved a tiny bit closer. "Would you like..." Another trail off. Another bit closer. "Would you like to..." She trailed off a third time. He was so close he could count the tiny wrinkles in her lips. Another breath closer, and their souls would collide as they fell into a tender, sweet kiss.

"Yes." He saved her from asking as he tightened his grip on her waist. "Yes, I would."

RIIIIINNNG! RIIIIINNNNGG!!!

The moment shattered. The possibility of a kiss died. Kate fled Clark's arms, diving across the room to collect her cell phone from the nearest table.

He never knew two hands could feel as empty as his did when Kate left him like that.

Chapter Fourteen

S haking so violently she almost dropped the phone twice, Kate scrambled to answer the call while trying to brush the stardust from her eyes. She almost kissed Clark Woodward. She wanted to kiss Clark Woodward.

"Hello?"

"Kate!"

Her lifelong friend Michael's voice couldn't possibly be mistaken for anyone else's, even when it was dominated by loud background noise. In the split second of his greeting, Kate picked out bits of sound with surgical precision. Laughter. A Santa going ho-ho-ho. Music. So much music and conversation everything mixed into a chaotic, cacophonous mud of sound.

"Michael? Where are you?" Kate pressed her free ear with a finger, hoping the closeness would help her hear his shouting voice.

"Are you still with Public Enemy Number One?"

"Yeah, he's in here with me. And don't call him that."

Kate didn't dare look at him. He'd wanted to kiss her, too. The very thought weakened her knees and blew on the embers inside her heart.

"Great. Get into the car and have him drive out to the location I'm texting you, okay? You should be able to get there if the roads in his backwoods are clear."

A ding from her phone alerted Kate to a text message. She glanced at the GPS signal Michael sent and furrowed her brow. A random spot in a random field.

"Why are we going there?" she asked.

"Just do it, okay? You'll see. Trust me."

"Okay... If you say so."

"Don't sound so glum! If this doesn't make him fall in love with Christmas, nothing will!"

"I'll ask him if he wants to go."

Fingers still shaking, Kate ended the call. They'd planned something, a secret kept even from her... what could they be up to?

"What's up?"

"Do you want to go on a little drive?"

Everything about him—his stance, his mouth half-opened and ready to ask a million questions she didn't have the answers to—told her he wanted to talk about what just happened between them. The kiss. Well. The almost-kiss. The kiss she desperately wanted. The kiss whose absence tingled on her lips. She could only hope everything about her told him not to push his luck.

"Yeah. Yeah." His head dipped in disappointment as he dipped out of the room. "Sounds good. Let me get my coat."

Ten minutes later, they sat next to each other in the front seat of the car. The GPS gave muted directions to Clark, who had to navigate by headlights because the back forty didn't have any lights to speak of.

"Do you know where we're going?" he asked, scrunching his face as he tried to see further ahead of them than the light would allow.

She shrugged and leaned into the impossibly comfortable seats of Clark's car. They needed to get there soon. Any longer in this quiet, dark, comfortable seat and she'd definitely be asleep.

"I don't know. Maybe they're having a bonfire or something."

"On my property? Without my permission?"

"I can't think of anything else they could be doing. It's a big, empty field."

Kate kept her arms firmly tightened across her chest and her eyes anywhere but Clark's direction. Pretending to be endlessly fascinated by the dark blurs passing them outside wasn't easy. It was, however, necessary. She didn't have the time to parse out her feelings about her impulsive desire to kiss him. She'd only come here to make him fall in love with Christmas and her town, not to make her fall in love with him.

"Maybe Santa's real and he's coming to personally give us our presents," Clark joked.

"Or maybe there's a freak snowstorm and we'll get to have a snowball fight."

"Snow in Texas? Better chance of Santa coming to town."

Another stretch of silence met those words as Kate didn't know what else to say. The only words she could come up with were: *I really like you and I want to kiss you, but I don't think it's a good idea because you're trying to destroy my town and maybe liking you means I won't mind if you do. I have to love my town more than I love you or I'll lose everything.*

An impulse moved her hand to the dark radio. Some music would distract them both. She almost pressed the power button before remembering his stern words against Christmas music this morning. They'd ridden in silence all the way through Miller's Point because he hated it; she didn't need to invite more conversation or conflict with a stupid choice.

"What's up?" he asked, when her hand retracted.

"Oh, sorry. I know you don't like the music."

A pause. Then:

"Go ahead. I don't mind so much anymore."

"Really?"

"It's growing on me."

And you're growing on me. As she turned on the radio and switched the dial to her favorite Christmas station, she kept that particular opinion to herself. It wouldn't make a difference anyway. She was going to show him the meaning of Christmas (somehow, and apparently with Michael's help), he was going to give them the company back, and then he'd be gone. Back to Dallas where he belonged. This would be nothing more than a memory. A cocktail party joke he could tell about that time he almost kissed a poor, provincial, Christmas-obsessed girl in Miller's Point.

But at least she'd have the festival, right? That had to matter more than anything, including this crush she'd fallen headlong into.

The problem with breaking the crush completely was that as they drove deeper and deeper into the darkness, Clark started tapping the steering wheel and humming off-key with her favorite song. *I'll Be Home for Christmas.* It was so sweet, so unexpected, she almost cried. And if she hadn't been careful, she definitely would have fallen in love with him right then and there.

"Well."

Upon their arrival, they found no bonfire, no Santa, and certainly no snow. They didn't even find a single other human being. Only a large, dark, grassy field.

"Are you sure we went to the right place?"

"Yeah. This is where the GPS took us."

Her illuminated phone was meant to take them straight to the coordinates sent her way by Michael, but he must have gotten them wrong. Or perhaps the dense forest kept the location services from working properly. Kate squinted at the screen and checked her roaming settings. No, this seemed to be the right place. Only, it couldn't be. There wasn't anything here. She shot off a quick text to Michael.

Why'd you send us out to a random field?

The three little dots appeared. A text followed shortly thereafter. *Walk to the edge of the hill. Overlooking town.*

"He wants us to look down into town, I think."

Miller's Point was something of a geographical oddity. More accurately, it was a linguistic oddity due to its actual lack of a point or nearness to a point. Essentially landlocked and settled into the valley between two high, forested hills, Miller's Point was a fraud. Miller's Valley was actually correct, though it didn't have quite the same ring to it. Kate led the way to the edge of the hill, less than fifty yards ahead of them. When the light from the car's front bumper finished guiding them, the ambient light from the town below led them the final distance, until they could see Miller's Point down below.

And that's when Kate realized Michael's plan.

"Wow." To her surprise, Kate realized she wasn't the one who said that. Clark did. Whipping her head back to see him a few paces behind her, she spotted him, illuminated by the light of the town, the image below reflected in his emerald eyes. "What is happening down there?"

In his official letter of dissolution of The Christmas Company, Clark demanded the immediate removal of all decorations from the town square. They were to be put in storage immediately. And to their credit, the grounds crew team of the festival, both paid and volunteer workers, all stayed through the night to get the job done. The only thing not packed away for storage was the Christmas tree itself, which stood unlit in the center of town. Not a single decoration accented the square. The only lights that should have been coming from town were the actual lights of the houses down below. People should have been tucked away in their living rooms or in their beds, ready to celebrate tomorrow's holiday.

Only, they weren't all tucked in their beds. They weren't silently waiting for the morning to come and the now private festivities to commence. The town square of Miller's Point was alive, as active and full as any evening of the actual festival. Without the decorations or trappings of the season, they made their own color and illumination. Tacky Christmas sweaters and red and green tights were lit by hundreds of white candles, held by singing people. Even here, high upon a hill just on the edge of their village, their voices rose up to Clark and Kate's ears.

Kate realized her misplaced cynicism in Michael. He hadn't organized this for their benefit. He'd been invited and wanted them to share in it. It wasn't a trick to get Clark on their side; it was a sincere expression of a town's faith.

O Holy Night
The stars are brightly shining.
It is the night of our dear savior's birth…

Their voices didn't ring out in perfect harmony. The song was at times too fast and at times too pitchy to be easily recognized as *O Holy Night,* but Kate's soul still moved with the music.

The lesson Clark was, no doubt, brought here to learn hit her just as hard. She'd been so certain Miller's Point needed the festival to stay together, never once considering that it wasn't the festival keeping them together at all. It was their love for one another. Nothing could break that, not even a businessman with a heart of steel.

"Do you…" His voice shook. A grumbling sound came from his throat as he attempted to no avail to clear it. "Do they do this every year?"

"No. This is the first time they've done this. At least, I've never seen it before, and I've worked with them since I was seven."

"So, they just came together on their own? To celebrate?"

"Yeah. I think so." When he didn't reply, she gave him a slight nudge. There was emotion in his eyes she'd never seen before, a fullness she didn't recognize. "Are you okay? Do you want to leave? Do you want *me* to leave?"

Clark ran a hand through his golden locks and stammered, two things Kate wasn't sure she'd seen him do.

"No, please. Will you..." He trailed off, voice thick with emotion. "Will you sit here with me for a while? I need to think. I want to watch."

At the edge of a hill that might have been the edge of the world, they sat in the damp grass, not caring how the wet seeped into their clothes. They shared in the awe of the sight before them. Clark promised to take everything from the people of Miller's Point. Kate promised to do everything to get it back. Yet, there they were. Spending the most sacred night of the year being in fellowship together, lifting their voices up and coming together as a community. There was nothing there but their love for one another and their belief in the goodness of this holiday.

Kate's humility consumed her. She thought she needed to save the world, but really...what was she doing? Trying to make herself the town hero? Trying to force herself into the center of a conflict that wasn't really there? Was she really so self-obsessed to think anyone in this town needed her? That it would die if she didn't save the day? She swallowed hard to hide the tears. She didn't want Clark to see them.

"What's wrong?"

Rats. Too late. Clark saw everything; Kate considered it his worst quality. Too perceptive. She sniffled.

"It's just beautiful, that's all."

Until now, they'd been sitting an honest distance apart. Close enough to feel his heat, but far enough that she thought he couldn't easily reach out and touch her. Another miscalculation. His warmth wrapped its way around her as his arm crossed her shoulders and pulled her into his side. At first, she resisted. But it felt so nice. Beyond nice to be held when she wanted to fall apart in her own shame. She'd lived in Miller's Point her entire life and still didn't understand anything about it. Collapsing into his side, she welcomed his chaste embrace. There wasn't a bit of harm or prowl in it. It comforted her.

"I've never seen anything like this."

"Me either."

"I thought it was just for the money, you know? A way to drum up tourism for a few months a year, but you all really love Christmas, don't you?"

"We love each other." All the ways she could think of to describe the sensation either fell short or sounded profoundly cheesy. Better to be accurate. "I think Christmas is just the excuse to love each other publicly."

The empty field whistled behind them, and their voices stayed in whispers. Being overheard was an impossibility here. Still, they couldn't help but confide in one another as though they stood in the middle of a crowded room. Time danced on the edge of a cliff while Clark's chest tightened and his heart hitched in his chest, a movement of muscles Kate heard loud and clear. Her head on his shoulder felt better than any pillow.

"I can't imagine loving anyone that much. Or

being loved by anyone that much. It's almost freezing, and they're out there singing."

"Really? You've never loved anyone that much?"

What a sad, empty life. Kate could barely imagine the darkness of a life lived unloved. No wonder he resented them so much at the start. Kate's nightmares could only conjure up who she'd be without the love of her town.

"My parents, but..." She marveled at the careful way he considered his words. Upon meeting him, she pegged him as the decisive, cold type who spoke and assumed his words would have the desired impact because he said them with such authority. "I think sometimes I forget what loving them felt like. Like, I buried it so deep for so long that it doesn't feel right anymore. I'm remembering a memory of a memory so I don't know if it's real or imagined."

From her place on his chest, Kate couldn't get a good view of him. Maybe it was for the best she didn't. He needed her compassion, but he didn't need her romance. Torn between his bewitchingly handsome face and her convicted town, she settled for playing with a loose thread on his hastily acquired overcoat.

"I think anyone's capable of that kind of love," she said.

"Even me?"

She'd never heard two words so filled with the promise of hope if confirmed and the threat of despair if denied.

"Especially you."

Neither of them were wearing watches. They didn't dare look at their phones. There was no way of marking time except for the passing of songs from the assembled crowd below. Kate and Clark remained frozen in their poses, two breathing statues carved from flesh and awe, entranced by the groundswell of spirit coming from Miller's Point.

"Do you want to go down there?" Kate asked as the music paused long enough for someone—Kate swore she recognized Miss Carolyn, with her fake antlers stuck on her head of silver hair—to walk up to the podium for a reading. Michael sent them up here to see the festivities, but Kate didn't want Clark to miss out if he wanted to join in. She hesitated to encourage it, just in case his presence sent a ripple of rage through the crowd, but wanted to offer all the same. "It could be fun to be right in the thick of it."

"I'm happy where I am, thanks."

He saved her from the freezing water. He tolerated Christmas, maybe even learned to like it… The dance. The almost-kiss. He wanted love. Her love.

For the first time in her life, Kate didn't know if she wanted to share her love with another person. A friendship was one thing, romance was quite another. Especially on Christmas. Christmas gave everything a Heaven-touched glow; it sang of forever.

Her thoughts tore at one another in a bench-clearing brawl as Miss Carolyn stepped down from the podium and the crowd returned to their singing.

I heard the bells on Christmas Day

Their old familiar carols play
And mild and sweet their songs repeat
Of peace on earth, good will to men.

"I don't know if I like that song," Kate said, scrunching up her nose. She never met a Christmas song she didn't like, but this one always rubbed her the wrong way. Clark chuckled, sending white puffs of warm air out into the dark night air. The temperature was dropping rapidly. Kate didn't know how much longer she could hold out before shivering took hold of her, especially after her dip in the river this afternoon. Billy McGee at the general store had sworn up and down this coat would protect her against any weather Miller's Point could produce. She'd have to call him up about his 30-Day Satisfaction Guarantee.

"Why? What's wrong with it?"

"Peace on earth, good will to men," Kate shrugged and finally sat up. After goodness-knew how long resting on his chest, she finally stitched herself together enough to support her own weight again. Instant regret flooded her. A chill a minute ago turned into full-on shivering with the sudden loss of their shared body heat. "They don't seem to care about women."

"I care about one of them."

A bolt of light broke the darkness around them, invisible to anyone but Kate. Her foolish, wanting heart wanted to throw herself in his arms and kiss him. It clung to that light, never wanting to let it go. Her frightened, skittish self retreated into the shadows.

Dangerous. Risky. Impossible. Loving Clark

Woodward was all of these things. She couldn't let herself want it.

"Clark," she admonished, pushing herself to standing. The more distance between them, the safer she'd feel. "You really shouldn't…"

"*Shouldn't?* I don't understand. All day you've been showing me what it means to love someone and now that I want to, you're saying I shouldn't?"

He followed as Kate strode closer to the cliff. Surely, he wouldn't follow her off a cliff? A hundred possible tactics flew at her and she grabbed hold of the first one she caught. Play dumb. Be obtuse. Deliberately obfuscate.

"You should care about everyone. All of those people—"

"I do care about them, but I don't… I'm not falling in love with them. I'm falling in love with you."

She froze at the edge. He stood behind her, not near enough to touch but somehow near enough to reach into her chest, grab her heart and hold it so tenderly the heat of oncoming tears burned her eyes.

"You barely know me."

"You don't feel the same way?"

"That's not the point."

It was as good as an admission, but she couldn't even think the words. She marveled at the ease with which she said, "I love you," and "love ya," to her friends and neighbors, only to balk now when something real and magical waited just three steps away from her.

"Then what is the point? You love so many people. Why not me?"

"...It's scary."

"I know." He breathed a laugh. "Why do you think I've been avoiding it for so long?"

His soft words coaxed some truth out of her, a stammering, hard-to-admit truth, but a truth nonetheless.

"When I love someone, I can focus on them. I can make sure they're safe and comfortable and happy. I'm very good at loving—"

"But not so good at being loved." The breath left her body. He soldiered on. "Because that means being vulnerable. Being taken care of. When was the last time someone took care of you, Kate? Or listened to you the way you listened to me today?"

He stood in front of her now, his back to the cliff's edge and framed by the light of the town below. Still, she stared at her shoes.

"What?" She could almost hear his hand flex with nervous energy. "Do I need to go find some mistletoe for you to look at me now?"

You can just run now. Run into the forest and call someone to come and find you. You could just jump off the cliff. A fall from this height probably wouldn't kill you. A body of broken bones only marginally less appealing than facing her feelings, Kate looked up.

"I see you," he whispered.

And I see everything about you, Clark Woodward. You have so much love and compassion bottled up, so

much you've hidden and want to give now you know how.
What if I disappoint you? What if I fail and don't live up
to the me who exists on December 24? What if the magic
dissolves on the 26th and you go back to Dallas and I'm
alone in a crowd again? She didn't ask any of those
questions. And he didn't answer. What he gave her, as
he closed the gap between them, was so much better.

"I never knew I could feel this way. I thought I
was trapped, but you opened my entire world up. And
filled my house with so many pine needles I don't
think I'll ever get them out."

"It's easy, you just take a high-powered vacuum
and—"

"You've made this stupid holiday into one of the
best days of my life. You made me feel something,
Kate. Do you know how long it's been since I've let
myself feel anything?"

"I'm happy I could help," she said, ever the
diplomat even as his nose almost brushed her with its
closeness. Her heart—oh, her poor reckless heart—
threw itself against her ribcage, banging to get out. A
strong hand landed on her right cheek. His pulse was
as fast as hers.

"Why did you come to my house in the first place?
And why did you stay?"

"I just didn't want you to be alone anymore."

"And I don't want to be alone anymore. But I don't
want you to be alone anymore either," he said.

A pause. A lifetime of happiness hung in the

balance of that pause. Kate said nothing. She didn't know how.

"May I kiss you?"

"Only if you want me to fall in love with you."

Chapter Fifteen

D espite what his boarding school roommates or overly friendly colleagues in the office thought, Clark had kissed women before. They never set his soul on fire as they seemed to do in the movies, nor did they live up to the locker room banter thrown around by the men in his acquaintance, nor was it a gentlemanly thing to do, so he never bragged about his romantic encounters.

Now, he thanked his past self for never inflating the memories or exaggerating the stories. They only would have cheapened the most perfect kiss in all the world.

His lips brushed hers, featherlight at first, not wanting to push his luck. Everything about her was soft, the perfect contrast to his rough edges and tough exterior. His hands moved to gently cup her face and he drew her lips into his for real this time. The slightest pressure, and the kiss exploded into a final firework of connection. His heart caught fire and his eyes were blinded to everything but her as she responded in kind. The kiss spoke louder than any words they could have said or wishes they could have made.

Given how much he despised it, he never expected the most important moment of his life to happen with Christmas songs being sung in the background. This morning, the moment would have been ruined by the inclusion of "O Come, All Ye Faithful." But then again, this morning, he wouldn't have fallen in love with Kate Buckner.

He was so glad not to be the same man he was this morning.

When the kiss broke—too soon, as far as he was concerned—the dark world brightened and he tipped his forehead against hers. Thoughts like stars hung around his head, too many to count or hold onto. He wanted to kiss her again and again and again and ask her everything about her life. Did she like gray or blue better? When did she last laugh so hard she snorted? What movie always made her cry? How did he start to make her as happy as she'd made him?

"Wow."

Clark couldn't count on one hand how many times before today he'd ever said wow. He added it to the list of things Kate inspired in him. He now understood how to let go of his need to seem above everything. He embraced wonder.

"Yeah." A disbelieving sigh came from her smiling lips. How many times had she been kissed? However many it was, he hoped she liked his kiss the best. He was a competitive type. "Wow."

Turning her so they looked out over the town again, Clark pulled Kate in close, throwing an arm over her shoulder again. He loved this pose. So protective. So close. In this position, she could listen to his heartbeat and know it was real, know she made it race every time she spoke. He swept his free arm across the glittering landscape of houses and businesses, all lit from the inside. Identifying with a building didn't seem a particularly smart thing to do, but Clark did all the same. Each of those houses looked so dark on the outside. Night painted their exterior walls. But their windows revealed the truth. The light within spilled into the streets, promising warmth and comfort inside. He felt like that now, trapped in night but carrying a raging fire in his chest. A fire Kate started.

"I think I see what you're talking about with this Christmas stuff now."

"It's amazing, isn't it?"

"It's magic."

"No." She gave him a little shoulder shove. The smile she no doubt wore echoed in her voice. "It's love. Better than magic."

"I don't like telling people they were right and I was wrong," he admitted. Kate changed his life, sure. She opened up new worlds of possibilities in just a day... Still, old habits die hard. In business, he never said sorry or admitted fault. He barreled forward without regard for those beside or behind him. With Kate, he wanted to accept her love of him and this holiday, but he wasn't sure if his lips knew how to form the words necessary to admit his fault.

"You don't have to tell me. I already know." By now, he knew any time she sounded smug, she was really teasing. He groaned anyway.

"That's even worse."

"Then go ahead. Tell me I'm right and you love Christmas now and you're a big fat softie," she punctuated those last three words with pokes right into his gut. "Who believes in miracles and that you deserve good things."

You deserve good things. The pokes to his gut didn't knock the wind out of him, but that sentence certainly did. A lifetime of neglect told him the exact opposite.

"I wouldn't go that far. I'm just not used to being given anything. Even though my uncle did try, I didn't *want* to be given anything. When I was young, I was always battling a ghost, you know? I worked myself to the bone at school and college and then at work because I needed to make my parents proud. I needed to carry on their legacy, and I had to fight every step of the way to do it. You're just giving me all of this, and it's... I don't know how to handle that." He stumbled over the words. Rolled his eyes. Old habits die hard, and one of his oldest habits happened to be not letting anyone into the inner workings of his mind. He'd lost countless girlfriends, friends, mentors and roommates that way. His last relationship ended with her saying she didn't want to be with him anymore because of his lack of emotional availability, to which he responded *yes, that's probably for the best.* Kate's presence threatened the fabric of his entire personality. "Look what you've done to me. I'm a sentimental mess now."

"You can be a sentimental mess. I won't judge."

"It's just that I care. My whole life, I just wanted to care about me and my own baggage and duty and responsibility. I didn't know how to care about other people," he declared, a little too loud but not afraid to let the entire world know his secret. "And now I understand what it means to. I care about you. And this stupid holiday. And your town."

"So," Kate breathed on his skin. "Do you think you could give us back the festival?"

"Come again?"

He hadn't quite heard her. Or, at least, he couldn't have heard her right. Why on earth was she still talking about the festival? They were together. The town clearly didn't mind functioning without the festival. They should have been walking on cloud nine, apart from every worry and care of the mortal, un-in-love world. She must have said something else.

"If you get it now, don't you think you could consider giving us the festival back?"

"I don't understand."

"You took it away because you didn't understand what it means. Now that you get it, I thought maybe you could, y'know. Help us out."

"Help you out."

He separated the words. Help. You. Out. Each of

the words, he understood individually. In that order, they no longer made sense.

"Yeah." She nodded.

"I didn't cancel the festival because I don't *get* Christmas," he explained. In one motion, he extricated himself from their sideways embrace so he could get a good look at her. He turned his back on the singing town. The skin just under his collar started burning. "I cancelled the festival because it's a financial liability."

"Right, but it pays back in what it gives to the town. And the people who visit. Like you."

His stomach dropped.

"Oh."

"What?"

He saw her clearly for the first time, and he saw himself. The world—spinning with joy only a minute ago—screeched to a slamming halt. Vertigo overtook him. He blinked to steady his vision.

Once, he'd gone on a field trip to a 3-D planetarium on a school field trip. The shock of taking off the glasses during the middle of an illusion had rocked him.

He felt that same way now. All of his illusions and understandings about Kate Buckner turned out to be nothing more than blurry projections, useless colors splashed on a paper-thin screen. Fake. Incorrect. Pathetic of him to buy into it. God, it hurt.

"I'm an idiot," he declared, meaning it in every sense of the word even as it stabbed him to say so.

"No, you're not."

"Yeah. I am." Swallow. Breathe. Don't raise your voice. Just state the facts. Letting go of your tight control over yourself is what got you in this mess in the first place. "You're a liar."

"Me?"

She had the good sense to balk at the accusation, but Clark didn't buy it, just like he shouldn't have bought anything she sold him all day. The first thing he would do when he got back to Dallas was head straight for the optician's office. Only a blind man couldn't see the con played out so deliberately in the lithe body of this beautiful woman.

"You're good, don't get me wrong. But how did I not see straight through you? You were using me."

"Using you?"

"Don't play dumb," he snapped. His entire body ached with the pain and the weight of it; it consumed him too much to keep from barking at her. "I see it now. You wanted to wrap me around your finger, giving me all of this garbage about not wanting me to be alone because you thought you could manipulate me. You made me start to...*feel for you* so you could use me to get your festival back."

"I didn't—"

"Not even a little?"

She stammered. Staggered backward. That told him plenty, but not nearly enough to bring him the pain necessary to break away from her. He'd need to hear it from her lips, to hear the confession of the betrayal before he could trust himself not to fall into her arms again. The irrational, stupid part of him that got him into this mess in the first place wanted nothing more than for her to tell him it was all a misunderstanding and explain how none of his suspicions were correct. The smart, detached part of him knew he needed to cut this cancer out before it infected all of him. He'd been right all along. Love—if it existed at all, and that wasn't even something he was sure of—was a tumor, not a cure.

"I wanted to be close to you."

One of his assets as a businessman was his ability to see a situation clearly and choose a plan of action. Kate's motives, cutting as they were, made perfect sense. They were logical. He saw the path through them clearly.

"So you could use me to get what you wanted. You are a liar." He repeated it and watched it slice straight through her. Now he questioned everything he knew. Were those tragic stories about her family even real, or did she make them up for sympathy? The ornaments, did she make up those stories about them on the spot? Did he know anything real about her, or had he been falling for a fiction this entire time?

"I'm not a liar. I just needed to do what was best for my town!" She raised her voice. Clark didn't give her the satisfaction of doing the same, no matter how much he wanted to, no matter how red his skin grew under his collar. Doing the best thing for her town was as good as a confession. Another one. She didn't give a lick about him. He was a useful, lonely idiot willing to believe any affection tossed his way after a lifetime of being starved for it.

"You admit it."

"But when I saw you at the diner, I realized you had never had what we had. I wanted to share it with you."

"Yeah. Because you wanted to use that to your advantage." The next revelation hurt the most. No one in his life ever liked him. But he was stupid enough to believe she might be the first. He'd fallen, all right, but not for her. He'd fallen for her trap. Hook, line and sinker.

"You convinced me you liked me."

"I do!"

Any better and she'd win an Oscar. The woman even managed tears. They puddled in her eyes, refusing to overflow. Clark paid them no attention. They were just another tool in her deception.

"You only stuck around because you had an endgame. Was all of this," He pointed an accusing finger down to the town. They still sung, the lemmings. "part of it, too?"

"No!"

"Convincing." Clark laughed derisively.

"Honestly, Clark." Her small hand flew to his chest, the pleading gesture of a woman broken by her own game. "This wasn't me."

One look down the ridge of his crooked nose and he removed the desperate hand. He never wanted to be touched by her again. If Miller's Point knew about her plan to con him out of his own company, they probably organized this entire thing to trick him. To give him a childish love of a stupid farce of a holiday so he would fall over himself to give them this expensive, two-month long game of Charles Dickens dress-up. Even if she didn't call this sing-along, she was complicit in it. As the mastermind of this scheme and the pied piper of Miller's Point and all her people, he felt no guilt in holding her responsible, not when his heart was the prize she'd incidentally managed to seize.

"Maybe not, but it was them. They were in on your plan, weren't they?"

"It isn't like that," she ground out between gritted teeth.

"What is it like then? Explain."

Her mouth opened and closed, invisible, soundless words came out, but nothing else. For the first time, Clark raised his voice.

"Explain yourself!"

Her shiver of fear would have made him feel like the biggest heel on earth if she hadn't started it.

"I wanted to get the festival back, yes. But I wanted to help you, too."

"Two birds with one stone, huh?" He snorted, crossing his arms to keep himself from shaking with cold. A cold winter night to reflect the cold heart of this woman.

"I'm not going to deny that Miller's Point is always my first priority, but I never lied to you. I want to be with you." Again, she reached for him. He backed away before she got the chance to touch him. "I'm falling for you. Please don't let this get between us."

"You're just saying that because I haven't given you what you wanted," he said, no uncertainty wavering his stern voice.

"No. I'm saying it because it's true."

True. She made countless spoken and unspoken promises today, and she'd broken every single one by lying to him. If she would go to these lengths to win back a stupid festival, what kind of person was she really, deep down in her heart? He thought of his parents. The stories he'd told her about them. He kept them so close to his heart no one ever saw or heard about them, yet he'd opened his mouth and blabbed his tightest held secrets. As much as he despised her in this moment, he hated himself the most. His lifestyle of cold calculation wasn't a bug; it was a feature that protected him from heartbreaking blunders like this one.

Why did this hurt so much? How had he given her so much power? He wanted to crawl under a rock and never re-emerge almost as much as he wanted to sell her beloved festival off piece by piece in front of her just to show her how spiteful and cruel he could be, in spite of her assertions to the contrary.

"I don't think you know what that word means. I opened up to you. I told you things I've never told anyone. For what? So you could use them against me?"

This fight began with his decision to remain rational and unattached, to tell her how badly she hurt him without ever allowing him to show her how badly this betrayal pained him. But the more he spoke, the faster his avalanche of anger grew. She'd quivered in fear when he raised his voice earlier; he wanted her to do it again.

"I did it so you could finally understand what it's like to have a friend."

No. He wouldn't listen to that line again. He wouldn't be a victim twice. She said this stuff because she needed him. He was nothing more than a pawn in her game, a piece she could move around to get what she wanted. The glory of having saved Miller's Point.

Did she even like Christmas? Or was her slavish devotion to the rituals and false promises of the season nothing more than a ruse, too?

"I don't need friends. And I don't need you."

"Clark. Please don't…"

"You know what, Kate Buckner." He spit her name. It would be the last time it ever crossed his lips and he wanted her to know how much he hated it in the deepest pits of his being. Once it was spoken, he straightened, pulling on the hems of his coat to give him a more dignified, regal appearance. He was once again the Clark Woodward of this morning, the Clark Woodward he would be forever. "You did make me believe in something today. Love or whatever you want to call it is just as fake as Christmas. And I don't want anything to do with it. I was right when I said I didn't care about you. I wish I'd listened to my gut."

"You're just saying that to hurt me," she said,

though the defense, like the flicker of compassion in her eyes, was weak. He turned his back on her. His car lay less than fifty yards away; he'd use it to head straight for Woodward House. Tonight, he could remain in the terribly decorated manor, a reminder of his failures, but tomorrow he would depart for Dallas and send an assistant in his stead. His direct involvement in the Miller's Point branch of Woodward Enterprises could easily be handled by anyone on earth besides him. He'd never come back to this place. They didn't deserve each other.

"And you just said everything you said to use me. If I hurt you, well. I guess we're even now."

He imagined she would follow him. Stay persistent. Turn him around and kiss him full on the mouth because she really did love him and he was being too stubborn or too blind to see it. He imagined a last-minute reprieve from the pain of losing her this way. It didn't come. A little voice almost got lost in the wind, and the crack of her boots against stray twigs and leaves signaled her departure from the scene and from his life. A fact he should have been glad for.

"Fine."

This time, when she went into the deep, dark forest of the back forty, Clark did not follow her. She and her stupid holiday could jump into a hundred icy rivers for all he cared. He was going home. He was going to take down the decorations. And he was going to go back to his lonely life. He would be alone, but at least he would be safe.

Being alone meant never having to open up to anyone. Being alone meant never having to take care of anyone. Being alone meant security. Tranquility. Ease.

Being alone meant no one could see tears trickling down his face.

Chapter Sixteen

K ate didn't get very far into the forest. The flimsy light on her cell phone couldn't contend with the creeping darkness and generally left her feeling like the first victim in a direct-to-video horror movie. Of all the ways she conceived of dying, she never dreamed it would happen in the middle of the Woodward family's back forty while crying over a stupid man.

A stupid, beautiful man whose heart she'd broken.

She paused in the middle of a circle of trees long enough to consider her options. All of her things sat back in Woodward House. Her wet clothes and toothbrush and the now ill-advised present she'd left for Clark under the tree.

Oh, the present. She'd give anything to be able to slip in through a crack in a window and steal that back before he got a chance to open it. Would he even open it at all? Or would he toss it in the nearest fireplace and watch it burn to ash? Her gift joining the embers broke her heart, but her gift would no doubt insult him. She couldn't decide which outcome she dreaded more.

No, she couldn't go back for her stuff. If he was any kind of man, he'd send it into town or send her an Amazon shipment of new clothes and toothbrushes. Any further encounter between them would be pointless. But she couldn't keep randomly walking through the woods in the dark. The mental Rolodex in her mind spun, searching for the least embarrassing person she could call to help her out of these woods—physical and emotional. Michael would be glib and make too many jokes about it. Emily would probably drive straight for Clark's house and beat the daylights out of him. In a town of less than ten thousand people, Kate knew there was only one woman she could call on for help.

"Hello?"

Miss Carolyn answered on the first ring.

"Miss Carolyn?" Try as she might, Kate couldn't keep the miserable sob from cracking the words. In the background of the other woman's side of the call, Kate could make out the general merriment of the town square. Like an ironic fairground soundtrack playing in the background of a melodrama, the carol singing and laughter creeping through the phone mocked her, underscoring her pain. "I think I need you to come pick me up."

Michael would've asked what was wrong. Emily would've asked who hurt her and what they were going to do about it. Miss Carolyn?

"Send me your location. I'll be there in ten minutes."

True to her word, no less than ten minutes later, Miss Carolyn's red pickup truck screeched into the muddy field where only a few minutes ago Kate and Clark watched the sing-along down in the valley. As she walked out from the forest towards the glow of the headlights, Kate reeled. To get this far from town that fast, she probably didn't even pause for stop signs.

Miss Carolyn ran to meet her, scooping her into one of her world-famous hugs. For the first time in her life, the woman's warm embrace did nothing to soothe Kate's cracked heart.

"You're gonna freeze to death out here," Miss Carolyn said. "Let's get you in the car."

"Yes ma'am."

Kate followed the older woman's lead. Her swishing silver hair glowed in the moonlight, leaving a distinctly witchy vibe in her wake. As grateful as Kate was for Miss Carolyn's rescue from the forest, the worry lines creasing her face dropped a pile of lead into the pit of her stomach. A pair of reindeer antlers sat crown-like upon her silver hair and a tacky Christmas sweater replaced her usual red flannel, a uniform Kate probably would have replicated if she hadn't spent the entire day falling head over heels for the perfectly wrong man. The initial appeal of calling Miss Carolyn was her sage advice, the wisdom she'd always offered Kate through her life. Now, Kate didn't want advice. She wanted to shut herself off from the world and forget everyone else existed.

They settled into the cab and took off into the night. The Woodward House was private, fenced-in land, but if anyone knew the way to sneak in and out through a broken or missing stretch of fence line, it was Miss Carolyn. That woman knew everything.

"You warm enough?"

"Yes ma'am."

Snuggling into the familiar tobacco and air freshener scented seats, her shivering finally subsided. Though she'd stopped crying a while ago, her face was caked with the salt from her teardrops, as if she'd been swimming in the ocean all day and forgotten to shower. Kate no longer wanted to sob and weep over Clark Woodward, but the salt cracking on her skin almost reminded her of armor.

She marveled, in the beginning, at Clark's ability to feel nothing. It frightened her more than anything; she swore she'd never let herself get to that point, where she so spurned the idea of feeling that she simply chose to avoid it all together. Tucked in the cab of Miss Carolyn's car, Kate realized the choice wasn't a conscious one. She hadn't decided to die inside. It just happened. Somewhere between hanging up the phone and finding her way into this truck, she just stopped caring. About everything.

What had caring gotten her? What had caring gotten Clark? A big, fat nothing.

"Want to tell me what happened?" Miss Carolyn asked.

"No ma'am."

"You sure?"

Kate squirmed. The day's events weighed squarely on her shoulders, pressing down until she feared they might flatten her altogether. Her heart—like the flat line of her voice—remained placid and unbothered, but the pressure on her back increased.

"No. I'm not sure," she confessed.

"Tell you what. Why don't we go to the square and get some hot chocolate and some songs into you—"

"No." Kate barked. Off of Miss Carolyn's shocked look, she attempted to recover. Just because she no longer cared didn't mean she had to forget her manners. She corrected herself. "No, thank you. Just take me to my apartment, please."

"Your apartment?" Miss Carolyn spluttered.

"Yes ma'am."

"By yourself? On Christmas?"

"Yes ma'am."

Eyes trained forward, hands folded in her lap, Kate didn't dignify Miss Carolyn with a response to her clear shock. She would not be deterred, even if the older woman gripped the steering wheel as if she drove the escape car from a botched bank robbery instead of through the empty streets of Miller's Point. Going to the town square to feign happiness as she sang lying songs about all of creation singing *gloria* appealed to her about as much as diving into a pit of live, starving snakes.

Her initial assessment proved incorrect. She wasn't actually empty or dead to the little voices interpreting her body's reactions into categories like sadness or rage. All of those things existed within her, they just couldn't be heard over the one dominating force controlling her entire view of the world at present.

Bitterness.

She was, plain and simply put, bitter.

"Are you feeling all right?"

"I failed," she said, twisting her hands together. Her voice was black coffee. Her eyes were probably darker.

"Oh, honey. You didn't fail."

Miss Carolyn's pity burned her, hot acid on her skin.

"I let everyone down. I tried to get the festival back and I failed."

"Michael and Emily told me about your plan."

"But that wasn't all. He was so broken." She placed a hand over her own icy heart. "Frozen. I thought maybe if he understood what I saw in this holiday—"

"He'd understand why we love our festival so much."

"No!" What had she done in her life to make everyone think she couldn't possibly really care about this man? Or did everyone, including Clark himself, think him so beyond redemption the idea of her trying to rescue him from a life of loss and misery was completely outside of the realm of possibility? "I thought maybe I could save him. I thought maybe he was just a Scrooge, you know? He needed to see the value in people. And himself. And he'd just open himself up."

To love. To me.

"What happened?"

Kate snorted. The more she encountered the memories she made today, the more childish she saw herself. She really thought she could protect a man's soul by putting up some Christmas lights and serving some turkey? What a dumb, naive girl she was.

"I was almost right. It almost worked. But I messed it up. He thought I was just using him. And it undid everything."

"Did you explain yourself?"

"Yes ma'am."

Miss Carolyn, in her capacity as Director of Festival Operations, always asked three questions in any dispute. What happened? Did you explain yourself? Did you apologize? For reasons unknown to her, the third question went unasked as they crept closer and closer to Kate's apartment. She readjusted her hands on the steering wheel. From the corner of her eye, Kate peeked long enough to see her press her lips into a thin line.

"I really think you should come to town and be with all of us. You shouldn't be alone tonight."

"Why? Because I'm a pathetic mess?" Kate bit questions with the irrational force of a rabid dog. Miss

Carolyn scooped her out of the freezing forest and brought her home. She wasn't her enemy. But Kate wanted to push her away; she wanted to forget her own foolish attempts to change her small slice of the world.

"No, because no one should be alone on Christmas Eve," Miss Carolyn echoed Kate's own words back to her just in time for Kate to say something she'd never before said. Not in her entire life.

"I want to be alone."

"A little company and a little cheer will do you good."

"It didn't do Clark any good."

"Then he's not worth your time."

Not worth her time? What happened to the *find the good in everyone* lessons their A Christmas Carol festival taught throngs of people every year? If Scrooge was meant to be redeemable, so too was Clark.

And if Clark couldn't be saved... If Kate failed... It meant everything she believed was a lie. Christmas. Love. Salvation. The fragments of her deeply held convictions crunched into dust beneath the weight of her newfound cynicism.

"We tell people things that aren't true, Miss Carolyn. We tell them this holiday has magical powers that can save anyone, but that's a lie. I don't want to go into town, okay? I don't want any cheer or any uplifting stories. I don't want to hear any more garbage about how people can change through the power of love. I want to go home and I want to sleep until January second."

"This isn't like you," Miss Carolyn said, her eyes as sad as Kate ever saw them. She ignored their sting and repaid their compassion with a stab of her own.

"We all have to grow up. Thanks for the ride."

The car hauled to a stop in front of Kate's building, and she practically threw herself out of the cab without saying goodbye. She lived in a tiny, closet-sized attic above the local bookstore, a fact she never minded and certainly didn't now. The room barely fit her and all her furniture; it certainly had no room to fit all of her fears and worries and memories and disillusions. In a place as small as hers, she could dive under her bed covers and forget the rest of the world.

Kate entered through a side door and climbed the rickety set of stairs up to her apartment. The attic had been divided into three sections by thin walls, separating out a kitchen, bathroom and bedroom. Even with the limited space—her bedroom, after all, had enough space for a mattress, a side table made out of a milk crate and a lamp—she'd gone all-out decorating for Christmas. Lights. Tinsel. Wreaths. The room reeked of pine and cinnamon. Kate's stomach turned, and she knew what she had to do.

With her foot, she opened the empty kitchen garbage can. Time to work. She started with the tinsel. Then the lights. Wreaths. Paper flowers. Finally, the miniature tree. They all met their fate in the bottom of the bin. After a minute of struggle with the lid, she succeeded in closing it.

Her apartment was clear. Clean of all Christmas foolishness and frippery. Now, instead of a sad apartment made merry by decorations, it was simply a sad apartment.

Too lazy to get undressed and into pajamas, she dragged herself into bed, peeling off only her coat before tucking herself between the covers. The place had no heat, which meant she never went to sleep with less than two layers on anyway.

Laying on her side, she found herself face-to-face with The Book atop her makeshift bedside table. *A Christmas Carol* by Charles Dickens waited there, begging her to open it and read it as she had done every year since she turned ten and saved up her pennies for this very copy. Its frayed edges and taped-over spine whispered to her, begging her to breathe in its tale.

Kate got out of bed. Picked up the book. And put it where it belonged. In the can with the rest of the trash. She was done with Christmas. She no longer had any use for its lies. Its betrayals.

Only then, with the last evidence of her belief in humanity safely discarded and the town outside her window still singing those blasted carols, did she return to her bed for a long, dreamless sleep.

Clark Woodward would curse the name Kate Buckner

until the day he died for making him feel this way. No, scratch that. For making him feel *anything*. As he drove back to his family's cold and empty home, he could think of nothing else than the new parameters of his existence. She'd opened up his heart and demanded he let everything flow freely both in and out of it, leaving him completely vulnerable to the pains of existence. Now that he'd broken through the dam, nothing could stop the flow.

It all rushed past him and around him and through him until all he could see was the road before him painted with projected colors of rage and pain and longing and sadness. Trying to push it away worked, but only for a few seconds at a time before it pinned him to the mat once again.

It only got worse when he arrived at the house and found the facade still covered in the remnants of Kate Buckner's invasion. He could no longer think of her as Kate, the girl he thought he fancied himself in love with. He could only think of her in formal terms, with a full, unbreakable name like a super villain. Lex Luthor. Inspector Javert. The Wicked Witch. To hold her personally and remember her humanity only broke him further because it was all fake, and he was a fool.

She and her team of scheming townsfolk rigged the Victorian-style manor with hundreds of flood lights and millions of tiny stringed lights, which brought out each painstaking holiday detail they'd hung outside. Giant wreaths, wrapped and bowed with red ribbons, hung between each of the fifty north-facing windows.

Two proud Christmas trees—decorated with identical gold baubles and red toppers—flanked the front doorway.

It was as beautiful as it was welcoming. As welcoming as it was sickening.

Clark yanked the car into park and jumped out. He wouldn't stay in a house like this. With the temperature rapidly dropping, he couldn't stay in the car either, but he could not stay in a house covered in the fingerprints of the woman who ripped out his heart, lit it on fire and roasted chestnuts over it.

Great, now he was describing things like she would have.

Storming across the frost-strewn lawn, Clark made a beeline for the first wreath on the first floor. Earlier today, she'd told him taking these things down would be an impossible job for one person. She lied about everything else. Why would she lie about this? He reached for the four-foot monstrosity and tugged. And tugged. And tugged. Until finally it let loose. The momentum shot him back a few steps until he tumbled to a halt, gripping onto the wreath for dear life.

With a minor success under his belt, he went for the rest. In a snowstorm of rough pulls and tugs, he yanked and pulled and ripped at each one in turn. By the fourth, his arms ached and when he fell backwards, he landed flat on his back with a face full of wreath pressing him down into the damp grass.

Fine. He could stay in this house for one night.

One night in a house where every ware reminded him of Kate Buckner wouldn't kill him.

It might break his heart even worse. It would no doubt keep him up all night. He wouldn't be able to escape the pain. But it wouldn't kill him.

He abandoned his pursuit of a fresh, un-Jack Frosted house. The wreaths stayed on the front lawn or at their window-side post and Clark took himself inside, where the fires Kate tended still burned hot and her decorations twinkled even more brightly as the night darkened and grew denser around the house. Room by room, Clark made the journey of extinguishing Christmas from the place. He took nothing down—he didn't want to touch anything, while the memories and pain burned fresh—but he unplugged the lamps inside tiny porcelain villages and flicked off breakers controlling scores of hung fairy lights. The formal dining room. The kitchen. The downstairs study. The hallways. One by one they fell to his power until Clark reached the closed French doors of the living room, the one room he'd been dreading all along. Where Kate told her story about her family and how much the festival meant to her. Where they watched *It's a Wonderful Life* and laughed at the plot holes while debating if George Bailey was a real romantic at heart. Where they decorated the tree.

Where Clark realized he was falling for her.

He considered leaving it, but knew it would only hurt worse in the morning. Might as well rip it off,

Band-Aid style. The doors spread for him, spilling golden light into the hallway.

All at once, his body deadened. He couldn't lift his arms. His feet refused to obey commands. His own skeleton revolted against him, forcing him to stand in the frame of the doorway and revel in all the ways he failed himself today. Ghosts of them together flitted around the room, teasing him with the promises of what might have been.

If he hadn't believed her. If she hadn't been lying. If he'd just listened to her explanation. If she'd said sorry. If. If. If.

Maybe he wouldn't have tried to tear down all remnants of her and maybe they wouldn't have spent Christmas apart from one another. Maybe he still would have believed everything she told him, about love and Christmas and all the rest of it.

But Clark learned long ago his life wasn't a movie and it didn't follow his whims or wishes. He was a sailboat at the mercy of its whims. All he could do was try not to capsize.

The fire. It needed dampening first. Then, he moved onto turning off the television, blowing out the candles, ripping down the mistletoe from the doorway. Piece by piece, he deconstructed her fairy tale until he stood alone in a dark room with nothing to guide his way but the bulbs on the Christmas tree. He ducked to unplug those too, but stopped when something strange tucked behind the tree caught his eye. A flash of red, sparkly paper caught the light, and he reached back to investigate. After a moment of grappling, he finally caught the hidden object and pulled it up to his face for inspection.

A small package, wrapped in red wrapping paper, tied with white and green curlicue ribbons. A practiced hand made the lines of the wrapping absolutely flawless. It could've been done by someone behind the wrapping department at Macy's, though Clark knew immediately only one person could've done this.

Kate Buckner. Kate Buckner had given him a present.

Clark couldn't remember the last time someone—not a business colleague, not a client or prospective partner—got him a present. Even his secretaries knew not to bother because he wouldn't open them anyway. Anything he got went straight to one of the lower-level directors who would no doubt enjoy tickets to the Cowboys game or a wine tasting trip for two more than he ever would.

Throw it away, reason said.

Open it, sentimentality replied.

For some stupid reason, he listened to sentimentality. For some stupid reason, Clark glanced up at the clock on the wall, checking to make sure it was *really* Christmas. Snake though she may have been, he didn't want to insult her by opening a Christmas present before Christmas morning. But at almost 1:30 a.m., it was most decidedly Christmas morning. Early, early in the morning, but morning all the same.

Rusty from years of not opening presents, Clark

struggled with the paper. At first, he attempted to lift the wrapping off at the tape lines so as not to completely destroy the stuff, but when the tape proved tougher than anticipated, he ripped straight through it, revealing the gift inside. It wasn't a box at all. It was a book. The red leather-bound cover gave no hints about the contents inside, so Clark picked himself off the floor and found a seat in his favorite chair by the now-darkened fireplace.

He opened to the first page, though the words were not type-written and official as he expected. Instead, a dark blue pen swooped cursive handwriting onto the first blank page.

Dear Clark,

The same compulsion telling him to light the fire and throw the book straight into it also told him to stop reading there, but his curiosity tamped down all of that. He read on.

Dear Clark,

> *I don't know you very well. Yesterday, we didn't exactly get off on the right foot. You want to destroy my town. I was rude and abrasive. We both made mistakes. But this morning, I saw you eating breakfast alone at the diner in town and my heart broke for you. Everyone in this town thinks you're a villain. And maybe they're right. But I*

don't think they are. And I'm hoping I can prove it.

Or, maybe better, I hope we can prove to you that you're not a villain. If, in the end, I fail to do this, I hope you'll read this book. It's made me see the best in people all my life. Maybe it can do the same for you.

Yours Most Sincerely,

Kate Buckner.

He parsed her words, picking them apart alongside everything he now knew about her. Everything in him wanted to stay angry with her, to cling to that pain that shot straight through him when she'd asked about the festival. It was no small thing for him to open up, so it was no small thing to be betrayed.

But...what if she *hadn't* betrayed him? The gift had been sitting there since her arrival that morning. She'd written all of this before they'd known each other, wrapped it with care when the last time they'd spoke he'd carelessly insulted her home and everything she cared about... Even then, she didn't think he was a monster. Even then, she saw good in him. And gave him something without any expectation of a return.

Clark sunk to the lowest pits of despair. She'd been honest all along. Sure, the festival was important to her, but this morning before she even knew him, she wanted to help him. He'd misjudged her character. He'd failed her, not the other way around. He would not cry. He would not cry. He would not cry. He just needed to see what was so special about this book. He sniffled, holding back his torrent of angst as much as possible. Delicate as he could, Clark turned to the title page and read the bold print declaring the name of Kate Buckner's favorite piece of literature.

A Christmas Carol.
In Prose.
Being a Ghost Story of Christmas.
By Charles Dickens.

Oh, no… He'd have to read this thing, wouldn't he?

Chapter Seventeen

Christmas Day

"Kate! Kate!"

To her profound disappointment, Kate Bucker did *not* sleep until January second as she'd been hoping. Groaning from her place under the blankets, she reached a single hand out and shooed whoever thought it smart to intrude this morning. No doubt word of her story and failure with Clark made its way around town by now—Miss Carolyn was many things, but discreet could not be counted among them—and she did not want to spend her new least favorite day of the year listening to her friends try to comfort and console her. For the first time in her life, Christmas Day would be hers to do with exactly as she liked. With no festival to plan and run, she could stay in bed until well past noon and listen to heavy metal or whatever it was anti-Christmas people listened to on December 25.

"Go away."

The security in her apartment didn't exactly rival Fort Knox. On most nights, since she didn't have a working lock on her front door, she usually kept a can with a bunch of coins in it directly in front of the door as a kind of makeshift alarm system. Apparently, she'd forgotten to put the can out.

Some mumbling voices, dampened by the comforter pulled over her head, didn't make enough sense for her to understand their words, but she did recognize the voices. Emily and Michael. Those two. The best friends a girl could have...except for when she didn't want any friendship. Petty though she knew it was, she wanted to wallow in her own self-pity, not accept it from anyone else. She'd always been the reliably cheerful, good ship lollipop kind of gal, but for once she had a real reason to disappear into her mattress. The mumbling stopped, only to be followed by the clicking of heels against hardwood and the sound of a closing door.

Wish granted. She was alone once more. Moments passed with no noise.

"Emily?" she called. No response. "Michael?" Again, no response.

The covers flew away from her body as she sat up and faced the day, but when Kate opened her eyes, something strange happened. Her little apartment didn't look as she'd left it. Decorations that had been shoved into the bowels of her trashcan—now crumpled—were placed back on her walls. Light shone through her windows though she could have *sworn* she closed the curtains before she fell asleep. Everything was almost exactly as it was when she woke up on Christmas Eve.

Why was her apartment back to normal? She shot up to sit in bed, giving herself a head rush. Spots appeared in her vision. She never slept well, so the sensation could almost certainly be caused by oversleep. The clock on the wall read 9:30. When had she *ever* slept that late?

It was then, as she checked the clock, that Kate noticed that something *was* out of place. There, on the windowsill, sat a book with a sticky note upon it. Sunbeams played on gold lettering.

"READ ME," it said.

A stubborn denial locked Kate's limbs. She recognized that book. Of all the books in all the world, it was the one she'd recognize anywhere. And she wasn't interested in reading it ever again. With a single bound, she was on her feet, ready to throw the book back into the garbage where it belonged—her best guess was that Emily or someone heard about her night and snuck in to make her feel better, a losing proposition—but then something hanging over her front door halted her stomping.

Her heart clenched. She gasped.

The Belle dress. The one she'd never gotten to wear after staying with Michael after he'd broken his leg, with its green velvet and perfect bustle, hung from a satin hanger over the lip of her door, complete with a corset, stockings and those shoes she'd always wanted to steal. Makeup and a curling iron, along with a plastic box of bobby pins and hair ties sat on her kitchen counter. Tacked to the dress waited another note, this time reading, "WEAR ME."

She had to be dreaming. She had to be.

Her fingers reached out to brush the lush material of the gown. It ran like water beneath her skin. Quickly, as if afraid someone would come in and take it from her, she held it up to her body and rushed to examine herself in the bathroom mirror. Yep. Definitely a dream. The Belle dress for the festival stopped fitting after her growth spurt in junior year of high school.

No. It wasn't a dream. If it was, she would have woken up by now. She didn't know who had gifted her this dress, but if the festival was closing and all its assets sold, she was going to get one good Christmas Day use out of this gown. Even if she hated the book from which it came—which she did—it was too beautiful to pass up. Her practiced hands flew through the motions of dressing and preparing herself. Years and years of helping Belles fit themselves in the fabric guided her until she looked the part. Victorian curls framed her face, crowned by a halo of holly, a customary feature of Belle's costume. Bright red lipstick brought some color to her otherwise pale skin. A red and gold brooch glowed at the base of her throat, pinned to the lace collar of her gown.

Oh, the gown. It fit as if it had been made for her. She spun, letting the skirts swirl up and reveal the petticoats and shoes hidden beneath. Even if everything was falling apart, even if her heart still felt half-stitched together, even if she didn't want to believe in Christmas anymore, her girlhood dreams were coming true.

She looked better than beautiful. And she felt it.

"Extra! Extra! Read all about it!"

Her vain inspection smashed to a halt with the intrusion of a squawking voice; it filtered through her thin window panes, a little, booming cry from the streets down below. Doing her best not to trip over her own feet—she couldn't remember the last time she'd worn heels that weren't her sturdy work boots—she scrambled for the window, stopping only for the briefest of moments to grab the READ ME copy of *A Christmas Carol* waiting on the sill. Costume firmly in place and book tucked under her arm, Kate opened the panes and looked down below, searching for the source of the newsboy cries.

Only, she didn't see the source. Not at first. Instead, an uncontrollable, unstoppable gasp flew from the depths of her chest as she stared out at the town square. It was there. Everything was there. As if Clark Woodward never demanded they take down the sets and facades and decorations, the square looked picture-perfect and ready for Christmas. As she leaned out of her window, she realized she was leaning into Dickensian England, with all of its beauty and wonder.

They'd put it back. They'd put it all back. She just didn't understand why. But there, on the corner between the facade of Marley and Scrooge's office and the butcher's shop, Kate spotted Susan Cho, a nine-year-old who played one of the Cratchit daughters in last year's festival. Dressed in one of the countless street urchin outfits Kate put together over the years, she held a newspaper high over her head. From this angle, Kate couldn't make out the headline or even if it came from Dallas or their stock of Dickens-specific recreations of London newspapers.

"Merry Christmas, London! Extra! Extra!"

"Susan! Come over here!"

As if she'd been walked through this a dozen times, Susan hustled down the block to stand beneath Kate's window, tucking the newsprint under her arm. If this were the festival come back to life, Kate would have scolded her for getting newsprint on the costume, but her confusion and awe at the entire situation overtook any practical thought. It didn't matter if the costumes got dirty or the fake newsprint smudged, not when there was so much outside at which she could marvel.

"Morning, miss!" Susan lisped through her two missing front teeth and tipped her newsboy cap. "What can I do for you?"

"What in the world is going on here?"

"Sorry, Miss Kate. Can't talk now. I have to stay in character," she stage-whispered before returning to her strolling and hawking. "Extra! Extra!"

For her part, Kate remained rooted to the spot.

"But if I *was* able to talk to you, I'd say you should come downstairs."

"What?" Kate whispered back, starting a complete conversation in hushed tones.

"You're supposed to follow me."

"Oh." Whatever was happening here, whatever character Susan was meant to keep and whatever was happening to this town, it was clear there was a plan and an order in place. Kate just didn't know them. But if she knew anything from a lifetime of working with and around children, it was to play along with their games. "Okay. I'll be right down."

She gathered up her skirts and did as she was told, skidding down her steps towards the town square. Once out on the street, following close behind the little girl as she hawked her papers, Kate couldn't contain her curiosity.

"Hey, Susan?"

"Yes, ma'am?"

The little girl must have felt Kate's distress radiating off of her because she dropped her character in order to answer. God bless children and their inability to pay attention to anything for more than ten minutes.

"Is this a dream? Am I dreaming?"

She didn't exactly believe she was dreaming, but it seemed as likely as Clark suddenly having a change of heart and giving her the festival back.

"Hmmm." The little girl tugged on her cap, considering the question. "I don't think so. If you were I hope I'd be wearing something much cuter."

Unconvincing as the argument should have been, it swayed Kate. After the events of last night, would this bizarre journey through Miller's Point be something she would dream about? Unlikely.

By Sherlock Holmes logic, it meant she was definitely, for real, walking through the festival facsimile of *A Christmas Carol* in a sweeping ball gown on Christmas morning.

Susan led her around the empty square, all while Kate puzzled out what little she understood about her surroundings. Dickens. Susan. None of it made sense, but she decided she saw no harm in playing along. Her heart broke yesterday. It couldn't re-break. Besides, the pieces were too small to be crushed into anything else. What did she have to lose?

When they reached the corner beneath Scrooge's house, Kate turned to Susan for instructions. Susan, for her part, tapped her toe on the sidewalk and stared up at the closed windows.

"What are we waiting for?" Kate asked.

"I'm *really* not supposed to break character, but—"

"You there, boy!"

System overload. Kate's processing power extinguished itself within one second of hearing that familiar, booming voice fill the square. Like staring at a box of puzzle pieces, she understood the picture in front of her in fragmented snippets. She knew that line. It was Dickens. No one knew A Christmas Carol better than she; it only took three words for her to identify his speech. And when Kate followed the conversation up and up and up the wall of the building she stood in front of, she was greeted by the unfathomable puzzle piece.

Clark Woodward. Leaning out of Scrooge's window. Wearing the Ebenezer Scrooge costume. Screaming Scrooge's Christmas morning lines.

Rats. Somehow the cut of the Victorian era costumes made him even more attractive. Great. Just great.

"What's the day today?"

Nope. Susan couldn't be right. This had to be a dream. Nothing else could explain it. Forget Sherlock Holmes logic. Not only was Clark wearing the Scrooge costume, but he somehow got at least one person in town to trust him enough to play along with… whatever this charade was?

No. Wrong again. If this was her dream, Clark would get the lines absolutely right instead of paraphrasing them. This was *definitely* happening, but why?

"Uh… Christmas Day, sir? What're you, crazy?"

Ah, Susan caught the paraphrasing bug, too. As the Assistant of Operations, Kate always stayed on book and gave the performers line notes at the end of each night, ensuring vigilance and protection for the Dickens text. This morning, protecting a long-dead author seemed everyone's last priority.

Kate knew everything there was to know about this scene. Pick any random scene in *A Christmas Carol*, she could have recited the dialogue, at least, entirely by heart while visualizing its exact place in their version of Victorian London. Here, after waking up very much alive, Scrooge renews his lease on life and decides to live every day as if it's Christmas, beginning by employing an errand boy to fetch him the biggest turkey in London.

What a crock.

Caught between her desire to continually roll her eyes every time they spoke and her rapture at watching the most wooden, stoic man in the world wildly shout about turkeys with a face-splitting grin on his face, Kate leaned against the nearest lamp post for support.

His smile, rare and pure, weakened her knees. Her last thoughts before falling asleep last night were, I'm so glad I got Clark Woodward out of my system, but the longer he smiled and the longer she stared at it like a snake charmer's victim, the more untrue that statement became. He hurt her. He hated her. But he was not out of her system.

Dickens's dialogue—or this interpretation of it—flew past her like a familiar song, allowing her to just drink him in. A dangerous prospect. If this was a dream, she'd dream something stupid like falling into his arms, and if this was real, she'd endanger her heart. And then probably stupidly fall into his arms.

Unable to speak during the performance, a hurricane swirled inside her. Remnants of her feelings for him yesterday swirled with her anger at not being able to fight them off well enough.

At the end of their scene, Susan took the oversized bag of gold coins and rushed off, leaving Scrooge and

Belle—Clark, who had somehow made his way down to street level, and Kate—very much alone, but that didn't break his concentration.

"I must go see the charitable gentleman. And Fred and his wife. Oh, thank you, Spirits!"

Apparently, these were cues of their own as out of nowhere, Doctor Joe Bennett appeared, dressed as the charitable gentleman Scrooge denies a donation earlier in the book. In real life, Joe played this role every year as a bit of a charitable scheme in and of itself. As the Chief Physician of the county's charity hospital, the festival always donated a little something to the cause. But when Clark approached him and shook his hand, he did not pull out one of the phony-baloney bank notes used during the regular festival. Clark instead handed the man a very real-looking check, and the man's shock wasn't the well-rehearsed expression he used every year during this big moment in the narrative.

"Hey, man…"

The line was most definitely, *Lord bless me!* Yet another clue the check in Clark's hand was real.

"And not a penny less. I owe you many, many back-payments, and this is just the beginning."

Doctor Bennett rooted himself to the spot, jaw nearly scraping the floor, while Clark-as-Scrooge hummed to himself and scooped up several brightly wrapped presents on his way down the slowly filling street towards Fred's house. Familiar faces of the town started to mill about in their costumes, just as they would any other Christmas morning. As if this all were very normal indeed. Without the slightest clue what else to do (she thought she might need to stay and give the doctor a dose of oxygen to combat the symptoms of his shock, or at least stick around long enough to see if the check really was real and how much it was made out for, but ultimately decided against it because she didn't want to get stuck taking care of a fussy doctor type), Kate followed them.

The scene in Fred's house always pleased crowds, and this morning was no exception. Kate giggled as Fred's wife fainted at the sight of Scrooge and Scrooge scrambled to help her—a comedic diversion not written into the original text, but added at a much later date by Miss Carolyn in order to beef up the character when Kate played it at sixteen—and followed along as Scrooge proceeded to collect people, imploring them to bring along foodstuffs and presents, treating them all with the charm and guile of a newly risen king. Such generosity, such goodness was an unnatural fit for Clark, but perhaps that was why the cautious parts of her hated how much she wanted to believe it.

In spite of her newfound hatred for this bogus holiday, the naive glass shards of her heart longed for him to be the real-life Ebenezer Scrooge. She wanted his smiles and his warmth to be real.

But it wasn't. And when she examined things more closely as Clark picked up small children and spun them around or joined in carols, Kate realized she didn't care for this at all. The spectacle was just that: a spectacle. Fake. Phony.

He had an angle. All of this was part of some plot. To humiliate her or to make fun of her or to stomp on her one more time... She didn't know. But he was working a fix and she wouldn't fall into its trap. With that, she folded her arms across her chest and resolved to give off the most unsympathetic, hateful, grumpy vibes she could manage.

Basically, she channeled him from one day ago.

"Can you show me the way to Bob Cratchit's house?"

All at once, he was there, directly in front of her, asking for directions to Bob Cratchit's house. Oh, yes. He was real. And so, so unfairly handsome. She'd never seen his eyes catch the light like this or his smile relax into an effortless assurance of his goodwill.

Kate urged herself not to give in. And she didn't. Something was going on here, and she could indulge it for the sake of her festival family, but she didn't have to invest herself in it. Blindly, Kate nodded and took the arm he offered her. Soon, she found herself leading a parade of Victorian-dressed characters carrying presents and goose, pies and wreaths like some kind of out-of-place drum major. Behind her, they sang in unison, a feature of their penultimate scene. They did it every year. This was the ending of *A Christmas Carol.* Clark, somehow and for reasons passing understanding, brought the end of the festival into his home and let it take life there.

The doors to the Cratchit House stood closed, and, against her will, a familiar rush of joy fluttered in Kate's stomach. Whether or not Clark knew it, this was her favorite part of the entire story. The beauty of the tale and the reversal of fortunes for the Cratchits made the entire journey worth it. In the novella, the confrontation between Bob and Scrooge happened at the office, but for the sake of bringing Tiny Tim back for one final "God Bless Us, Every One," they transposed the encounter to Bob Cratchit's house instead.

As Scrooge always did—Kate would know, she'd trained six different Scrooges—he waved away the crowd, they feigned hiding, and he settled an angry scowl upon his brow before knocking upon Cratchit's door. *Boom! Boom! Boom!* Goosebumps raised the hairs on her arms.

She just hoped she wouldn't break and cry. She always cried at this scene.

The Cratchit family generally consisted of a real-life husband and wife and whatever children could sit still the longest and memorize the most dialogue, but when the Cratchits appeared today, Mr. and Mrs. Isaacs were not standing there in their costumes, ready for their close-up. Kate's breath hitched.

There, framed by the holly-lined doorway, stood Michael and Emily, dressed up in the poor clothes of the clerk and his wife, while the usual suspects of children cowered behind them at the mean ol' Uncle Scrooge. The last time Emily got in front of a crowd, she picked up the lid of a piano and vomited into it, so her appearance here caught Kate off guard.

If she had a heart any longer, it would have warmed and stretched with love for her friend's courageous appearance, made all the more amazing by her genuine acting chops.

"Bob Cratchit!" Clark-as-Scrooge boomed. "You did not come in to work today."

Michael cowered, his knees shaking in a mockery of knocking together.

"But it's Christmas."

"I never gave you the day off."

"You did, sir." To his credit, Michael appropriately stammered and stuttered over the words forcing them out between his teeth with all the joy of poisoning himself. He even wrung his hands. Kate couldn't have directed this scene any better. The children in the back did their part, too, huddling together as their mother grew in anger. "You just said to be in earlier tomorrow."

"Oh, I'm going to throw the book at you, you lazy layabout!" Scrooge shouted, shaking his walking stick for emphasis. Kate would have directed against that particular choice, but hamming it up seemed to be Clark's style of the day, a noted change from the man who wouldn't even smile at a little boy yesterday after he begged him to do so.

"Lazy layabout!" Emily charged forward, her thick curls shaking under her bonnet. She shoved up her sleeves as if to instigate a fight. Kate almost laughed. Almost. "I'll have you know—"

"I'm going to give you everything I've got!"

"Please don't! I'll come in now! I can—"

Scrooge cut him off.

"I'm going to raise your salary."

"Pardon?" Emily and Michael said at once, a unified explosion of shock.

"I'm going to raise your salary and take care of you and your family for the rest of my days. And," Clark waved his hands, calling the crowd from the shadows, filling the room with rich aromas and colors the likes of which contrasted deeply with the Cratchits' costume design, as was Kate's plan when she helped pick those outfits. The sight of the swarm of well-wishers sent Kate's temperature skyrocketing. Her stomach turned. "We will discuss the entire thing over the most beautiful Christmas dinner ever brought forth in the whole of Christendom!"

A cheer. Little Tiny Tim leapt into Scrooge's arms and he lifted him high upon his shoulders.

"Mr. Scrooge!"

The room filled, leaving Kate distinctly apart. A viewer of this spectacle. The object of their collective stare as much as they were an object of hers.

She wanted to vomit.

What on earth could have possessed them to all come here and be a part of this? Maybe it was Miss Carolyn. Surely Clark didn't do this all by himself. Miss Carolyn must have threatened to throat punch him if he didn't comply. They were trying to fix her Christmas cheer, surely. Or bring her back into the fold after a tough night of disillusionment and Clark was a part of that. They all bought into the dream, a dream she no longer knew how to be an active participant in.

Next in the story came the "Scrooge was better than his word" speech. Another surefire "Kate always cries at this part so make sure someone has Kleenex handy" moment.

It felt like Christmas. It looked like Christmas.

And she couldn't stomach it. She didn't know what Clark was doing in the middle of all of this. She didn't know what his game was. She didn't know what he wanted from her or why he seemed intent on hurting her through the one thing she used to love most in this world.

All Kate knew was that she needed to get out.

Chapter Eighteen

Clark spent half of his morning memorizing this Dickensian text, only for the woman he memorized it for to storm out of the house before he could even get halfway through his final speech.

The door of the Cratchit house slammed behind her, silencing the small living room as fifty heads turned to him in hushed anticipation. Paralysis set in, even as he clung to little Bradley, who waited patiently on his shoulder for his final cue. For a moment, the room could have passed for a ride at one of those high-priced theme parks, where the guests floated through fantastical scenes with broken animatronic characters who could only blink and jerk their heads. The heat of the room's bated breath left beads of sweat on Clark's forehead, trickling down his forehead as his only indication of the passing of time. He couldn't wrench himself away from the closed door; the place where Kate once stood now tortured him endlessly. The absence of her ripped at him; a punch in the gut would have been less painful and robbed him of less breath.

After too long a silence for the little boy's taste, Bradley clonked the top of Clark's head with his cane, a new brand of pain almost bold enough to shake him from his stupor.

"Hey." Clark blinked. Another clonk. Bradley addressed him in a stage whisper through clenched teeth, a manner of confidentiality he probably mimicked from a million Saturday morning cartoons. "Hey, Mr. Clark. I think they're waiting for you to say something."

Michael caught Clark's eye first, a small miracle. After staying up to read his present from Kate, he tracked the young man down. A frantic phonebook search later and he had both Emily and Michael in the living room of Michael's cabin, where he told them the entire story. Being the sort of guy who never spilled his guts, Clark struggled, but eventually explained everything.

They didn't get on board with his plan, however, until he told them the entire truth. *I think I'm falling in love with her and I don't want to lose my one chance because I was too blind to see that some people are good people.* Halfway through the Dickens book, Clark started to understand why he'd been so happy to assume the worst of Kate, even when everything she said and did instructed him to believe the best.

He couldn't believe what a jerk he'd been.

Once Emily and Michael got on board, they went

to work buttering up Miss Carolyn who did *not* care for him, expressing frequent and blatant desires to punch him in the throat. In the end, she only agreed to the entire scheme because Emily convinced her it was the only way to save Kate from her disillusionment...

Well, that and Clark allowed her one free punch to his stomach. The old woman had surprising strength for her age; no doubt a bruise started forming almost immediately. The rest fell together at Miss Carolyn's instructions. She yanked children out of bed and hustled parents into costumes. They organized a feast and reset everything in the town square.

And by the time the clock struck nine that morning, everything seemed poised to work. Clark would win the girl, save the town, and give them all the Christmas they deserved.

Only...it didn't work. Kate stormed out before he could even tell her the good news. Before she even had time to hear his apology. Or fall in love with him again.

"All right, everyone." Clark cleared his throat, a strangled sound as his trachea contracted and tightened. "I'm going to go—uh, to go investigate."

Depositing Bradley—who gave him an unsubtle wink and thumbs up once he landed safely on the ground—Clark bolted. He didn't know how to lose her like he'd lost her yesterday.

The streets and buildings around him blurred as he picked up speed (no easy feat in the Ebenezer Scrooge costume, which rarely saw this much physical activity), and he blew past every door and obstacle on his way. Even if she was halfway to Argentina by now, he was determined to find her.

Determination went unrealized when he skidded to a halt in front of the gazebo in the dead center of the town square, where he found Kate, facing away from him, sitting in a puddle of skirts on a set of wooden steps. She flinched as his footfall hit the wood a few paces behind her.

"I don't have a car and these heels are killing me. That's the only reason I'm still here."

It was then he realized she hadn't been shaking with noiseless sobs, but fooling with the difficult laces of the Victorian heeled boots on her feet. From directly behind her, he couldn't tell the difference, but once he stepped to the side, he saw the fight firsthand and the determined way her teeth dug into her bottom lip. In the cold, her skin both paled and reddened at the same time, the high contrast giving her an otherworldly glow amid the thousands of lights strung up across the square from the buildings on either side of them. Clark didn't want to think about the electricity bill they'd rung up over the last few days.

"Can I sit down with you?" he asked, pointing to the sliver of space between the end of her billowing skirt and the side railing of the gazebo's steps.

"Why?"

Good question. A smarter man might have gotten down on his knees and begged forgiveness. Right?

Clark didn't watch many movies, so his vocabulary of romantically tinged apologies was severely limited.

"I was hoping to talk to you," he said. A cringe bunched his shoulders together just beneath his neck. He'd never done anything like this; this limb upon which he was reaching out bowed under the weight of his own insecurity.

"You can't talk standing up?"

His chest tightened. After his cold dismissal of her last night, he didn't blame her. She had every right to despise him. Knowing the right was hers didn't make it hurt any less. He'd orchestrated this entire Christmas miracle for her, to make her feel better, not worse.

"I can, but you seem pretty upset."

"Well, I'm not."

"I've never seen you like this."

"I'm fine."

He could hit himself. Everything out of his mouth turned out to be the exact wrong thing to say.

"Okay. Okay." He breathed in a deep lungful of country air. Dallas never smelled this good, nor did it ever crackle inside him like the first spark of a fire. It cleaned him from the inside, clearing his head. A path presented itself, so he took it. A risky move, but one he had to take. "I'll just stand up here until you're ready to talk."

One of the few memories of his mother he held close to him was a story she used to tell about a woman who was separated from her love, and she sat by the banks of the river every day waiting for him to return.

His mother held it up as an example of true devotion, sacrifice and love. Though he hoped she wouldn't, he would wait a lifetime if Kate asked. Out of his own selfishness, he'd caused her pain; the least he could give her was devotion and a little bit of patience. He counted the minutes by the twinkling of the timed, dancing lights overhead. One cycle. Two cycles. Three cycles. And finally:

"Fine. You can sit down."

The space between the hoops of her skirt and the side railing barely fit, but Clark sat on an angle to speak to her, only to open his mouth and find he had nothing to say.

"Kate. I think—"

Good thing he hesitated. An explosion of hot air and frustration flew from Kate's lips, pouring out steaming accusations as she gesticulated wildly. Though it was hardly the time or place to do so, Clark couldn't help but store away Kate's habit of talking with her hands as one of his favorite quirks of hers.

"What is it with you, huh? Why are you doing this? What is all of this about? I don't understand."

A reasonable question, one he wished she'd asked before storming out of the house and out here into the cold where she would almost certainly catch her death only one day after he saved her from it.

"I got your present."

"Present? What present?"

Slipping out of his coat, he pulled a red-bound book from the breast pocket, which he handed to her.

Distracted by the slender volume, she barely reacted to him as he laid his coat over her shoulders and wrapped his red scarf around her throat. He took pains to brush her skin as little as possible, a task that proved almost impossible and left him with tiny electric shocks every time they *did* touch.

"The one you left under my tree yesterday."

"Oh."

As reverent as opening a prayer book, Kate turned over the pages until she stared at the title page engraving, a picture of an old man with a small boy on his shoulder. Clark didn't concede to wearing old age makeup as Emily suggested, but if he had, he and Bradley would have looked almost identical to the picture she traced with her red-painted nails now.

"*A Christmas Carol*," she muttered.

"Good title."

His quip went ignored as she thumbed the pages. Clark tried to rescue the moment.

"No one's ever seen me before. Or wanted the best for me. And you were right yesterday when you said I took your Christmas away, so...I thought it was only fair I try to give a little bit back to you."

"Why? Because you want to rub it in my face or what? You hated me yesterday."

"I was wrong."

"Yeah? Maybe I was wrong, too. I liked you and you treated me like dirt. You thought I was trying to manipulate you when all I wanted was the best thing for everyone." She'd long since given up trying to take off the uncomfortable shoes. Curling up under herself, she drew her knees into her chest, making herself as small as possible. Clark couldn't begin to see a way out of this. He'd taken a willful, loving woman and broken her like he'd been broken. The whispers in town were right. He was a monster. Kate sniffed and turned her head away from him, resting her head on her knees. "All I wanted was for everyone to be happy."

"I know. And that's what I didn't understand. I've never known someone who genuinely wants good things for other people. I wanted to be right. I think I wanted to believe you were only out for yourself and your town, that you didn't really care about me at all."

"Why?"

Another breath. Deep. Calming. Since putting down the book last night, he framed most of his decisions by following Scrooge's example. It took courage to admit his own fault and apologize to the Cratchits. Clark needed to find some courage of his own. With gentle fingers, he tugged on the end of his red scarf. Kate took the hint and turned her head back towards him. It still waited on her knees, as if her misery weighed too much to keep her head upright, but it was a step in the right direction.

And if this was the last time she'd ever let herself get caught dead in his presence, at least he'd have one last chance to look at her beautiful, bewitching eyes.

"So I could stop feeling things for you. So I could put you in a little box and forget you. Because I've never been in love before and falling in love is terrifying for someone like me. I like being in control. I like knowing exactly where I'm going and when I'm with you... You've turned everything upside down for me. It scared me. It still scares me, but—"

Once he started talking about her, he found it impossible to filter himself, but one purposeful look from those striking eyes silenced his rambling.

"I've never been in love before either."

"Really?"

He found it hard to believe on two levels. One: no one in the world carried as much love inside of her as Kate Buckner. How in the world had no one ever unlocked it and treasured it before? Two: she'd never fallen in love before and yet she chose him? Impossible.

"No better time than Christmas, huh?"

A dreamlike haze settled across her face, only to be torn away with a shake of her head.

"No. No." She held up her hands, brushing away invisible cobwebs. "You're not smooth talking your way out of this. I have to protect myself."

Yesterday, Clark would have shouted. Been indignant. Rejected her and all she stood for. Today, he slid down to the step below where she was sitting so he could look up at her, all while softening his sympathies.

"I'm sorry. Is that what you want to hear? I'm sorry I pushed you away. I'm sorry I shut you out and threatened to take away everything you love out of spite. And if you never want to see me again, I will walk out of this town forever but I can't do that until

I know I've made it right. Until you've had your Christmas and until you know you've changed my life."

"That sounds a little dramatic," she said, even as she hugged his heavy wool coat closer. He didn't blame her for thinking it a bit farfetched. When had a man ever changed in one night?

Oh yeah. In *A Christmas Carol*.

"It's not dramatic. I mean it. I wouldn't say it if it wasn't true."

You saw me yesterday, he implored silently. *You saw me when I couldn't even see myself. Please see me now.* Unlike Clark, she only hardened, a caustic undertone taking over her entire being as she tightened her arms across her chest. Did she feel the need to hold herself together? Did she feel as close to shattering into a million tiny pieces as he did?

"You're telling me you did all of this so you could get me back? Like…to win me?"

"No, I did all of this so you'd know you changed me. After what I did…" Clark loved the way she talked with her hands. When it came to his own twitches and ticks, he despised the way his hands flexed, an instant tell at how nervous he was. "I know I don't stand a chance. I have too much to learn about being a good man to deserve someone like you. I just needed you to know and leaving a sad voicemail at 2:30 in the morning wasn't splashy enough." Kate fiddled with her velvet skirts, but Clark spied her blinking furiously.

Did she have a tell of her own? "Now can I ask you a question?"

"One," she conceded.

"Why are you so upset? I know I hurt you, but you stormed out of *A Christmas Carol*, and I honestly thought that was the one thing you'd never do."

With a furrow of her brows and a sigh telling him she only answered because she promised she would, Kate laid herself bare. At this point, he couldn't tell if he made any progress with her or if she only hated him all the more now for all of his confessions.

"Last night, I swore off of you. And Christmas. So, to wake up this morning and be here with all of this," she motioned to the green dress gracing her body. When Clark saw it on the rack, he couldn't help but think, *is that really the dress she obsessed over?* He understood the appeal as soon as she waltzed into his view. She made a plain green frock glow brighter than any emerald. "It sort of makes me feel like Charlie Brown. The second I start believing in you, you'll pull away the football and I'll be on my behind wishing I had never tried at all."

"I'm not going to pull away the football." In a moment of stupid bravery, he placed one of his hands atop hers. "I swear."

"Can I tell you a secret?"

"Do you trust me with one?" he asked, afraid of the uncontrollable undertones of bitterness in the question.

Her hand moved beneath his, sending up red flags

and storm warnings in every corner of his body. *She's taking her hand away. She hates me. She's going to tell me to get lost and I'll be stuck with this big, dumb, broken heart.* Then, she turned her hand over and properly held his. The tender gesture grew his heart three times bigger than it had ever been before. Though she stared down at their intertwined fingers, Kate's growing smile couldn't be hidden behind her curtains of curls.

And with four words, she changed him forever.

"I really like you."

A brass band took over his heart. Fireworks replaced his pulse. Christmas really was magic. Scrambling back to sit on an equal step with her, Clark prayed this wasn't a dream. Or if it was, he wanted to live in this dream forever.

"I really like *you*," he replied. She tried to hide her smile, something he couldn't possibly attempt.

"And that was..." She paused so long Clark thought he would die from waiting. This time, she gave him the privilege of viewing her entire face; the shy smile reddened her already flushed cheeks. "That was a really good apology."

His jaw dropped. He'd been convinced she'd run him out of town on a rail.

"Was it?"

"Yeah, but I have one question."

"Shoot."

Anything. Anything. I'm all yours.

"Why am I in this ridiculous costume?" she asked, ruffling the skirts with a laughter-tinted huff.

A moment of panic. Clark remembered her telling a story about outgrowing the Belle costume—her favorite—so he arranged for it to be let out and altered by Miss Carolyn. Had he gotten it wrong?

"What? Don't you like it? I thought you said Belle was your dream role in the festival."

"It is, but..." Kate sighed, her fists wrapping into the velvet. "But..."

"But what?"

"But Belle and Scrooge don't end up together."

No sooner had she spoken than she scrunched her face in humiliation, slapping a hand over her face to cover the spreading blush. Adorable. Kissable. His heart opened wide to her.

"I've got news for you." He tugged her hand away from her face and tipped her chin up. "We aren't Scrooge and Belle." He pressed a kiss to her forehead. "But we can be. During next year's festival, if you want."

"Next year's festival?" The halting words left tracks of white air in their wake as her warm breath spiked the freezing wind around them. Unspoken hope brought out the muted green flecks in her golden eyes as she looked up at him. Clark knew how she felt. Desperate to believe, terrified to be disappointed.

"Next year's festival," Clark confirmed, jumping to his feet and taking her with him by their interlocked hands. "And you can make that call because you, Miss Kate Buckner, are the new Director of Festival Operations for The Christmas Company."

"Me?" She choked on the word, yanking her hand back so she could place it firmly over the place where her heart beat, presumably to keep it from running out on her.

"Miss Carolyn's looking to retire. She wants to enjoy the festival as a guest next year, and she recommended you for the job." The idea came to him this morning when Miss Carolyn complained about hurting her back moving one of the props around the town square. She muttered something about getting too old for this, and Clark offered her a generous retirement package. Apparently, she'd been wanting to quit for some time but didn't have the money. Now she did, leaving an opening for an upstart Christmas fanatic to take over. "I don't think there's a person in the entire world who would lead this company better than you."

Even when presented with her dream job, Kate stayed hung up on one thing in particular. She held his hands so tight he wondered if she was trying to keep herself from flying into the clouds with joy. He certainly was.

"You aren't ending the festival?"

"You were right all along. The festival is good for the soul. Even if it loses Woodward Enterprises a few dollars every year."

In the grand scheme of a billion-dollar company, that's all it was. A few dollars to make people happy and sustain an entire town? Yeah, now Clark saw the appeal of such a setup. Kate swallowed hard.

"I don't know what to say."

He pulled her close.

"Say you'll make next year the best Christmas ever."

"Nothing could ever beat this one."

Her head rested on his chest, where he hoped it would always remain.

"Miss Kate Buckner, would you do me the honor of giving me a second chance?" All of a sudden, music struck up from the bandstand at the far end of the square, grand and sweeping, as Clark ordered. The finale was meant to happen at 10 o'clock sharp, and a check of his watch affirmed Miss Carolyn's devotion to timeliness. "And dancing with me?"

"I'd be delighted."

They swayed in the cold air, accompanied by the roaring band down the street. Completely content. Completely at peace. Clark never knew such happiness. Not in his entire life.

As the song barreled towards it climax, Kate's eyes widened in awe and she pulled away from his chest so she could open herself up to the heavens.

"Snow!" she exclaimed, another delicious smile overtaking her bright features.

"Yeah," Clark confessed. "I told them to turn on the fake stuff. I thought it would add to the atmosphere."

"No, Clark." Kate took his hand and opened it to the sky. "It's not fake. It's really snowing."

Sure enough, one by one, tiny flurries landed on his palm before melting into his skin. This wasn't the sticky soap bubble snow or the false stuff covering every surface of Miller's Point to give it the illusion of snow. This was the real thing.

"Snow in Texas on Christmas Day," he marveled.

"See?" Kate returned her head to his chest. "Miracles do happen."

And for the first time in his life, as he danced with Kate Buckner in a gentle snowdrift, Clark Woodward believed.

The End.

Sweet Potato Biscuits
with Country Ham
A Hallmark Original Recipe

In *The Christmas Company,* Kate and many other people in town surprise Clark with a lavish Christmas feast. It includes every holiday treat imaginable—including sweet potato biscuits and ham. Our recipe would be a brilliant use of leftovers from your own holiday meal, and a perfect main dish for a Christmas brunch or lunch.

Yield: 10 servings
Prep Time: 15 minutes
Cook Time: 20 minutes

INGREDIENTS

Sweet Potato Biscuits:

- 2¼ cups flour
- 2 tablespoons brown sugar
- 2½ teaspoons baking powder
- 1 teaspoon kosher salt
- ½ teaspoon baking soda
- ½ cup (1 stick) unsalted butter, cold, diced into pieces
- 1 cup cooked mashed sweet potatoes, chilled*
- ¼ cup cold buttermilk

- 14 to 16 ounces sliced country ham (about 2 slices)
- 1 tablespoon butter
- as needed, honey
- as needed, country Dijon mustard
- as needed, blackberry preserves (or apricot preserves)
- as needed, butter

DIRECTIONS

1. Preheat oven to 450°F.

2. To prepare sweet potato biscuits: combine flour, brown sugar, baking powder, salt and baking soda in a food processor bowl fitted with a steel blade and pulse to blend. Add cold butter pieces and pulse until mixture resembles coarse cornmeal.

3. Add mashed sweet potatoes and buttermilk to flour mixture and pulse just until mixture comes together and forms a dough.

4. Turn the dough out onto a floured work surface. Gently knead just until smooth; pat into a circle to a thickness of ¾ to 1-inch. Using a 3-inch biscuit cutter, cut out biscuits. Arrange on a baking sheet lined with baking paper. Gather left-over dough into a ball, pat into a circle and cut out remaining biscuits (recipe makes ten 3-inch biscuits).

5. Bake for 15 minutes, or until golden brown, rotating the baking sheet halfway through baking.

6. While biscuits are baking, cut ham slices into 2 to 3-inch pieces. Melt butter in a heavy skillet over medium heat; add ham pieces and cook on each side for 2 to 3 minutes, or until sizzling and golden around outer edges.

7. Split sweet potato biscuits horizontally, layer

ham on bottom halves of biscuits and close with top halves. Arrange on a serving tray with choice of condiments.

* Recipe uses left-over plain unseasoned mashed sweet potatoes. Or roast a whole medium to large-size sweet potato (enough to make 1 cup of mashed sweet potato, without the skin) at 400°F for about 1 hour or until tender; cool, peel off skin and roughly mash sweet potato.

Thanks so much for reading *The Christmas Company*. We hope you enjoyed it!

You might like these other books from Hallmark Publishing:

Journey Back to Christmas
Love You Like Christmas
A Heavenly Christmas
A Christmas to Remember
Christmas in Evergreen

For information about our new releases and exclusive offers, sign up for our free newsletter at hallmarkchannel.com/hallmark-publishing-newsletter

You can also connect with us here:

Facebook.com/HallmarkPublishing

Twitter.com/HallmarkPublish

About The Author

Alys Murray was born and raised in New Orleans, Louisiana, and will always be a southern girl at heart. A graduate of New York University's Tisch School of the Arts, she travels with her fiancé as much as she can and writes as many love stories as she can.